Sixty-five

Sixty-four, Sixty-five

a novel by
Norah McClintock

Canadian Cataloguing in Publication Data

McClintock, Norah
Sixty-four, sixty-five

ISBN 0-7710-5446-7

I. Title.

PS8575.C62S58 1989   jC813'.54   C88-095068-4
PZ7.M33Si 1989

Printed and bound in Canada

McClelland & Stewart Inc.
The Canadian Publishers
481 University Avenue
Toronto, Ontario
M5G 2E9

For Michael

1

*N*ot many black people lived in St. Jacques in 1964. Cally Wright had lived her whole life there, sixteen years now, and had never seen one up close. She hadn't even seen one from a distance. People in St. Jacques tended to be white and, except for the old part of town, the area clustered around an ancient stone church, where the little stores had wooden floors and names like Brisebois or Arsenault or Gingras, people in St. Jacques were Anglophones. There was one Jewish kid in Cally's whole school; the rest were white, Anglo and Protestant. White Anglo Catholics went to their own schools. So did Francophone Catholics and, she supposed, Francophone Protestants, although she had never actually heard of a French-speaking Quebecker who was anything but a Catholic. But for sure there were no black people in St. Jacques.

Until now.

Cally sat on the front steps of the tiny house she shared with her mother and her little brother, and watched as the moving van unloaded furniture under the careful direction of a woman who was definitely black. Cally had seen the man too. He had gone into the house as soon as the van had pulled up, and he hadn't come out again.

There was also a boy. He was tall and slim and dark, with a headful of kinky hair that Cally couldn't tear her eyes from. She wondered what it felt like. Was it as wiry as it looked? It seemed to her that hair that kinked like that and stood up like that must feel like steelwool. But she didn't know for sure, and she wasn't about to go over and ask him if she could touch it. God, he'd think she was a lunatic or something. So she just sat on the concrete steps as the morning grew warmer and warmer, and listened to her transistor radio as she watched the people moving in.

She gazed across the street. Nothing was happening. Nothing ever happened in St. Jacques. There was nowhere for anything to happen. The whole suburb consisted of street after street of boring houses filled with boring people who followed the same boring routine day after day. And August was the absolute worst time of the year in St. Jacques. By mid-August everyone had been vegetating all summer, everyone was getting restless, and the only reprieve in sight was another year of school.

Mr. Curran was coming down the street. Cally checked her watch. Exactly ten o'clock. She sighed. Mr. Curran was a perfect example of everything that was wrong with St. Jacques. At precisely ten o'clock every morning all summer he had come strolling down the street in a pair of tan Bermuda shorts, a cap covering the bald spot on his head, and one arm yanked out straight in front of him by Casper. Casper was Mr. Curran's German shepherd. So far as Cally knew, Mr. Curran walked Casper at precisely ten o'clock every morning of his life; Cally just wasn't around to experience the thrill of this absolute sameness day after day. Most of the time she was locked in a classroom, learning useless dates and meaningless equations, stuff she'd probably never remember once she finished school.

Mr. Curran drew even with the moving van; he glanced at it, then at the woman who was standing beside it, then at the boy who was standing up on the shaded porch. Cally could see the sombre straight line that was normally his mouth curl down into a scowl. He scowled at the woman, then he scowled all around the neighbourhood. And then he saw Cally.

Cally groaned. Oh, God, he's coming this way. She started to fiddle with the dial on her radio, twisting it minutely this way and that as if she were determined to make the sound come in clearer so she wouldn't have to actually talk to Mr. Curran. She never knew what to say to him.

She heard the jingle of Casper's chain coming closer and closer, and then a cap-shaped shadow fell across her bare feet. She had to look up; she knew he was there, and she knew he knew she knew.

"Good morning, Mr. Curran," she said, and smiled a smile she didn't feel. That was one thing she resolved to change almost every year. That stupid smile that was plastered to her face all the time, no matter how angry or hurt or embarrassed she was, or how much she didn't like the person she was talking to or how bored she was. She hated it when people came up to her and saw that smile and said, "Hey, Cally, what's so funny?" It was *so* embarrassing, especially since she never had anything particularly amusing to say in reply. She only had her beet-red face and her stupid smile; the same stupid smile she was giving Mr. Curran now.

"Good morning, Cally," said Mr. Curran. He stood on

the asphalt driveway about six feet from her, one arm looking like it was being wrenched out of its socket. Casper was straining at his lead so hard, pulling and tugging, trying to get a whiff of Cally. Cally hated that. She didn't like it when dogs jumped up and tried to smell between her legs. She hated it when they slobbered all over her hand. And she didn't trust Casper one little bit. There had to be a reason the Currans' yard was surrounded by a five-foot-high chain link fence; and there had to be a reason that whenever Casper was allowed out of the yard, he was always securely chained to the end of Mr. Curran's arm.

"Nice weather we're having," Cally said at last. It wasn't all that nice. It was too hot and too sticky. But she couldn't think of anything else to say, and people Mr. Curran's age seemed to love to talk about the weather, mostly in grumbling tones.

"Too nice, if you ask me," said Mr. Curran, nodding in the direction of the moving van next door. Cally frowned. She had the discomforting feeling that there was something in what he said, like a shard of glass hidden in a pudding, but she didn't know what it was. "Weather's too nice up here if it starts attracting people like that," Mr. Curran said. "Wait until they get a taste of our winters, eh, Cally? Maybe then they'll get the idea."

Cally stared at Mr. Curran. She had never actively disliked the man the way Luce seemed to. Luce said he was stupid and old-fashioned and didn't know the first thing about kids. But to Cally he had just always been. He and his wife and his daughter, who was in university, had been living on the street before Cally had even been born. The Currans had known Cally's father and they were kind to Cally's mother. Mr. Curran's daughter had often babysat for both Cally and her brother. Mr. Curran was just a fact of her life, a neighbour around whom she had always felt vaguely uncomfortable. Her discomfort was more acute now, and she didn't know what to say to him. So she widened her smile fractionally and gazed down at her toes.

"Is your mother at home?" Mr. Curran said next.

Cally shook her head. "She took Walter to the pool."

"Does she know about this?" Mr. Curran asked.

Cally nodded. But if her mother had known that the new neighbours were black, she hadn't actually mentioned it to Cally.

"Tell your mother I'll drop by later," Mr. Curran said. He jerked on Casper's leash until he got the German shepherd moving. Cally breathed a sigh of relief as they loped back down the driveway. Then she glanced again into the neighbours' yard. The boy was standing closer to her now; he wasn't on the porch, he was on the lawn, right on the other side of the low cedar hedge that divided the two properties. And he was staring right at her. Cally smiled. The boy didn't. He just stared and, after a while, he turned and walked away, back across the lawn and into the house.

Luce stretched her bare legs out in front of her and arched the rest of her body backward. The swing began to move. She tucked her legs in and thrust her torso forward. Backward and forward. Backward and forward. Soon she was airbound, her thin tanned legs reaching for the leaves on the tree way in front of the swings. God, she felt good. The commercials were right. If you only have one life to live, live it as a blonde. If the guys hadn't been right out there on the playing field just beyond the swings, she would have whipped out her pocket mirror and taken another peek at herself.

Her mother had freaked, of course. But then, her mother freaked over everything. When Luce plucked her eyebrows, her mother freaked. When Luce shortened her skirts so that they were above her knees, her mother freaked. When Luce glommed on the eyeliner and the mascara so that her eyes leapt off her face the way a *Vogue* design leapt off the page, her mother freaked. So it was no big surprise when she started screaming the minute she saw the new, improved Luce. Bye-bye, mousey brown hair: hello, blonde bombshell. Now the trick was to get Pete to notice.

He was out there. She watched him catch a long pass, tuck the ball under his arm and, head down, charging like a bull, weave in and out of the other players, on his way to score a touchdown. At least she was pretty sure it was a touchdown. God, the thing about boys was they liked such dumb stuff. Put a guy out on a field with a ball, any ball, football, baseball, basketball, and he'd go crazy trying to score a homerun or a touchdown or a basket. And the rougher the game, the better. They loved to jump on each other in sweaty heaps. A guy who limped off the field was some kind of hero. A guy who *caused* another guy to limp off the field was a *man*.

Pete was different. She was sure of that. Sure, Pete liked sports. He was the star of the basketball team. He was tall – God, she loved tall boys, she'd rather die than go around like Sandy MacLean, all six feet of her, which was bad enough, a girl being six feet tall, but Sandy was actually dating a guy who was five feet tall. Pete was taller than Luce by a good seven inches. Plus he was handsome. Thick chestnut hair that curled tightly to his head. Dark-grey eyes, like storm clouds gathering. A deep, husky voice. Muscles a girl could die for; the guy rippled when he walked. And lately, very lately, he had started flashing little smiles at her. Which was why she was down at the park at such an ungodly hour on a weekday summer morning when there was no school. A guy who smiled at her the way Pete did just had to be interested in more than sports.

Pete played football every morning with a bunch of guys. And Luce made a point of just happening to be in the neighbourhood whenever he did. At first she had made Cally and Carolyn come with her. But then she'd read in *Seventeen* that even the most macho guys can be shy. So, to show off her new look to best advantage, she had ventured into the park alone, claimed a swing, and was just ever so casually swinging on it, not paying the slightest attention to the game going on. Well, not so that anyone would notice.

After an hour her back and her legs started to ache. She stopped pumping and let herself drift to a stop. "Stupid jocks," she muttered to herself. They'd rather chase a stupid ball around the park than spend any time with girls. She dug her naked toes into the sand and stood up. Well, to hell with them then.

Ohmygod! They were coming off the field now. The game had broken up, or at least paused for a minute. Some guys flopped onto the grass on their backs or stomachs. Some bent right over, their hands resting on their knees, panting. Pete peeled his T-shirt off and wiped the sweat from his face with it. His muscular torso was deeply tanned and slick with sweat. As he mopped his face, he looked up at Luce. Her knees turned to liquid when he smiled at her. When he started to walk towards her, she thought she would die right there on the spot.

"Hi," he said when he got closer. He had a big grin on his face. "So, it is you, eh?"

Luce could feel her cheeks reddening under her blusher.

"Some of the guys, they thought it was some new chick in town. Me, I thought you'd gone in for a paint job."

Death would be a merciful alternative to this, she thought. In fact, death was the only alternative to humiliation like this.

"Figured you'd see if it was true, huh?" Pete said. He was blotting the back of his neck with the damp T-shirt and squinting at her, still grinning.

"I don't get it," she mumbled. She couldn't look at him. She just couldn't. But if she stopped looking at him, he'd think she was even more of a jerk. If she was going to come out of this alive, she had to tough it out. Try to bluff him, like, what the hell did she care what he thought.

"You know what the commercials say. Blondes have more fun. Thought you'd try it out, eh?" Only he wasn't saying it the way she had expected. There wasn't a sneer to it, not even a tease. He just kind of said it.

"Yeah," she said.

He nodded and smiled at her again. "It's nice," he said.

Her eyes immediately doubled in size. "You think so?"

"Yeah. I mean, I wouldn't go out and get mine done on account of it. And it's kind of weird to think about doing it, you know, dyeing yourself another colour. But, yeah, it looks good."

She beamed at him and drew herself up a little straighter, so that he could see how thin she was, and how short her skirt was.

"Thanks, Pete," she said. She meant it.

"So, do they?"

"Do who what?"

"Do blondes have more fun?"

She laughed this time. "I've only been blonde since last night. I haven't had a chance to find out."

"Gee," said Pete, "that's a shame. Hey, why don't you and me find out together? Tonight. Maybe we could go see a movie."

"You and me?"

God, if the motion picture academy could see her now, how hard she was fighting to keep the squeal out of her voice, how she had to force herself to keep her pose, hands on hips, and not jump up and down, they'd have given her an Oscar in a minute.

"Yeah, you and me."

"Tonight?"

"Yeah."

She nodded. "Yeah," she said, "I think I'm free tonight."

"Careful, Carolyn," her mother said for the twelve-zillionth time that morning. "That's my best lamp you're carrying."

Yes, Mother dear, Carolyn muttered angrily under her breath. I'll be very very careful not to smash your stupid ugly lamp to smithereens, even if you are ruining my whole entire life. After all, what was one miserable life compared to her mother's best lamp?

"That goes in the front room," her mother said. "We'll take that awful old thing of Greatgran's down to the basement . . ."

"Mom, we've moved practically all of Greatgran's house down into Greatgran's basement. I don't think there's any room left down there."

"Don't be silly," said Carolyn's mother. "It's a very large basement."

"It's an even larger house," Carolyn muttered. But she set her mother's lamp down carefully in the corner and picked up her great-grandmother's lamp. Or, rather, tried to pick it up. The thing weighed a ton, it almost wrenched her arm free of her shoulder socket.

"It's solid brass," her mother said with a little smile. "Maybe I should help you."

"I can manage," said Carolyn sulkily. She hated this whole moving thing, and there was no way on God's green earth that she was going to pretend she didn't. If Grandma Dell was so worried about Greatgran, why didn't *she* take her in? Why was she making Carolyn's mother do it instead?

Carolyn wrapped both hands around the base of the lamp and, with a heavy grunt, hoisted it off the floor. The minute she had it up, she almost dropped it again, Greatgran's shriek startled her so much.

"Thief, thief!" Greatgran was screaming. Then she swept her arm around in an arc, almost bowling herself over with the force. "Thieves, you're all of you thieves!"

Grandma Dell swirled in from the kitchen, surveyed the scene with small, sharp eyes and said, "For Heaven's sake, Mother, get a grip on yourself. Those aren't thieves. That's Elizabeth and Carolyn. They've come to live with you."

"Live with me?" Greatgran stared at Grandma Dell.

"Mother, I explained it to you a hundred times," said Grandma Dell. "You need some help around the house.

16

And now that Elizabeth is on her own, she's decided to go back to school."

"What do I care what she's doing?" snapped Greatgran. "This isn't a school. If she's going to go to school, what is she doing here?"

Carolyn shook her head and set the lamp back down. This had been a bad idea from the start, and it was getting worse by the minute. Not only did Carolyn not want to be there, but her Greatgran didn't even want her there. In fact, Greatgran didn't even like Carolyn. The past few years, whenever Carolyn and her mother would come to visit, Greatgran would do one of two things: either she would spend the entire time peering at Carolyn with foggy, suspicious eyes, or she would quite simply ignore Carolyn, pretend that she wasn't there. In both cases Carolyn felt embarrassed and unhappy and was always glad when she and her mother said their good-byes and went back to their own little apartment. Now, however, there would be no place for Carolyn to go.

"Elizabeth can't afford to pay rent *and* go to school, Mother," said Grandma Dell. "Going to school isn't like working. They don't pay you to go to school . . . "

"I know that!" snapped Greatgran indignantly.

"So she and Carolyn are going to live here. That way you can help them and they can help you."

"I don't need help."

"Yes, you do," said Grandma Dell wearily, as if she had said it all a hundred times before. And with Greatgran's poor memory, Carolyn didn't doubt that she had done precisely that. "You need help. You're old."

Greatgran pulled herself up very straight and tall and sniffed the air. Looking Grandma Dell in the eye, she said, "So are you."

Carolyn burst out laughing. She couldn't help herself. It was so funny watching the two of them, both of them so old and wrinkled you couldn't possibly think of them as mother and daughter, they were more like aged sisters.

Greatgran turned very slowly and fixed Carolyn with a piercing stare. Carolyn clamped her mouth shut; she could feel her cheeks burning. Greatgran glowered in turn at Grandma Dell and at Carolyn's mother. Finally, she turned and shuffled slowly to the back of the house where her room was. Greatgran lived exclusively on the first floor of her three-storey house. The stairs were much too hard for her to negotiate.

Carolyn's mother watched her go. She sighed heavily and turned to Grandma Dell. "I don't know, Mother," she said. "Maybe this isn't such a . . . "

"It's necessary," said Grandma Dell sharply. "She's getting worse, Elizabeth. She doesn't know where she is half the time. And you know I can't look after her . . . " She broke off and threw a sharp glance at Carolyn. "Didn't your mother ask you to take that lamp downstairs, young lady?" she snapped.

"Yes, ma'am," said Carolyn, her own voice a little too sour.

"Carolyn." A warning from her mother.

"Sorry," muttered Carolyn. Her mother could make her say it, but she couldn't make her mean it. And she didn't.

2

Nothing to do. The curse of summer. Carolyn wasn't around. She was moving, poor thing. It wasn't like she was moving to another continent or anything. She would still be going to the same school, and actually, to look at it in a positive light, it was a step up to be moving out of that crummy little apartment she and her mother had shared and into her Greatgran's house with that enormous back yard. God, imagine the parties they could have in that yard. And Carolyn could do stuff she'd never done before, like just walk out back to sunbathe rather than having to go to someone else's place because you could never get any sun on that stupid little balcony they had at the apartment. Of course, Cally knew Carolyn didn't see it that way. Carolyn saw it as a blight on her life. Whenever Cally tried to cheer her up by pointing out the good things about the move, Carolyn would just roll her eyes and say in a cranky voice, "But it's my *great*-grandmother's house!"

The way Carolyn put it, there were major disadvantages to living in your great-grandmother's house. Like, old people didn't like loud music so Carolyn wouldn't be able to crank up the radio every time a Beatles song came on. Of course, Mrs. Quaid, Carolyn's mother, never let Carolyn crank the radio up to full blast anyway. But you couldn't tell Carolyn that, and still expect her to be rational about it.

Another big disadvantage Carolyn saw to her new living arrangements: she'd have to watch her Greatgran eat. "She never wears her dentures!" Carolyn wailed. "She says they pinch her or something, so she never wears them and whenever she comes to visit, Mom has to puree her food for her. Can you imagine? Sitting across the table from someone who's eating pureed carrots? Or pureed beets?"

"Obviously, you're an only child," Cally had said on that occasion. She remembered quite vividly what it had been like watching Walter eat, with pureed green beans and pureed lamb smeared all over his face, and pureed peaches finger-painted all over his high-chair tray.

"Yeah, well, imagine Walter ninety years old, all wrinkled up, and still acting like that," said Carolyn. In the end, Cally had to admit that she did see Carolyn's point. It would be kind of gross.

"Plus," said Carolyn, and Cally could tell by the tone in her voice, the thrust, the build-up, that this was a big PLUS, "she's totally ga-ga."

"So what?" said Cally. "I thought you said she's always been totally ga-ga. The stories you told, they were always like jokes."

"That was *before*," Carolyn said gloomily.

Cally guessed that a joke ceased to be funny when you had to share bed and board with it.

Anyway, Carolyn was moving today, so that put her out of the picture. And really, when you came right down to it, the only other person that Cally ever hung around with was Luce. And she didn't really like Luce. She would never trust her with a major secret. She only hung around with Luce because for some reason Luce and Carolyn had always been good friends.

It was weird. Everyone thought of them as a threesome. Luce and Cally and Carolyn. The Three Musketeers, that was what Luce's father called them. All for one and one for all. Except that Cally was pretty sure that Luce was only for herself. A lot of times Luce would do stuff like invite Carolyn over and not Cally. And a lot of times Carolyn would go with Luce and if Cally would venture to say, hey, how come you guys didn't ask me along, which she seldom did because it was always so scary waiting to hear what the answer was going to be, Carolyn would kind of frown and say, oh, Luce said she did ask you but you said you couldn't come.

Cally liked Carolyn. She really did. Carolyn was basically honest and she was kind of funny and she always listened to what Cally had to say. She actually seemed to like Cally. But when Carolyn went with Luce like that and then said what she said when Cally asked her about it, Cally was never really sure whether Carolyn was lying or not. And most of the time she felt bad for even suspecting Carolyn of lying.

She never felt guilty for suspecting Luce of anything.

Luce was one of those people who was always kidding around. She was flashy, wore the shortest skirts, the most makeup, the most outrageous clothes. She knew all the newest dances and songs and groups. She was thin and attractive – at least, she knew how to give that illusion with her makeup and the way she dressed – and she always made sure that everyone knew she was there. A lot of girls at school would look at Luce and think, gee, I wish I could be like her. Except that they were mostly the girls who weren't so thin, whose mothers wouldn't allow them to wear short skirts and pots of makeup, who couldn't manage to look good even if their mothers *had* been more liberal; in short, the girls who lined the walls of the gym at school dances or who, even worse, danced with other girls. The girls who had boyfriends looked at Luce differently.

Anyway, there was no way she was going to call Luce and ask if she wanted to go down to the village or something, only to have Luce totally humiliate her by yawning into the phone and saying she'd love to but she had to wash her hair. Or paint her toenails.

No way she was going back in the house either. Not to listen to any more of what Mr. Curran had to say. He had called her mother earlier and asked if she would like to come up and have a drink with them before dinner. But Walter had come back from his swimming lesson flushed and feverish and her mother didn't want to leave him. So, because Mr. Curran had seemed so disappointed, she had invited Mr. and Mrs. Curran and their daughter Susan, who was at home for the summer, down for drinks at their house instead. Then she had spent the rest of the day throwing together some canapés for the Currans' arrival and racing around looking after Walter, who hadn't vomited but was whining all the time.

Now the three Currans were lined up on the couch in descending order of age and size, the female Currans with their heads turned to the right, gazing at Mr. Curran as he explained the gravity of the situation to Cally's mother.

Cally had listened for a while, becoming increasingly

impatient when Mr. Curran kept referring to the new neighbours as a "situation."

"What does he have against them?" she asked her mother in the kitchen as she handed Cally a second platter of canapés.

"It's because they're coloured," Cally's mother whispered back. "Mr. Curran is very . . . well, old-fashioned."

"Old-fashioned?" She'd never heard it referred to in that way before. Cally carried the canapés back into the living room, then asked if she could be excused.

"Well . . . " said her mother, looking doubtful.

"But of course, Cally," said Mr. Curran. "I'm sure a young girl has other things on her mind, less serious things." He stood up when she left the room.

Cally had gone out onto the back porch and down the steps into the yard. She stretched out on a chaise longue and rubbed suntan lotion onto her arms and shoulders and onto the slice of stomach that her tube top did not cover. She squeezed a blob of lotion onto her knees and rubbed it into her legs. Then she had leaned back and closed her eyes.

She heard a screen door squeal; she turned and saw the neighbours' back door open and a figure step out into the sunlight on the small rear porch. It was the boy. The one Mr. Curran had been going on and on about. Cally got up from the chaise. She glanced towards the house, and could see Mr. Curran's head in the window. If Mr. Curran were to glance out the window, he would see her. Cally smiled.

"Hi, there," she called to the boy on the porch on the other side of the hedge. She began to walk towards him, smiling broadly, hoping that Mr. Curran *would* look up, *would* see what was going on.

The boy turned and stared at her. There was no smile on his face, none in his eyes. He stared at her white legs, her white belly, her white arms. Then his eyes skipped behind her. Puzzled, Cally looked to see what had caught his interest. But there was only the chaise, a small white table and the container of suntan lotion. She turned back to the boy.

"My name's Cally," she called. "Cally Wright."

The boy stared at her a moment longer, then he cleared his throat loudly and spat into the grass beside the porch. Maybe he'd been going to do it anyway. She'd seen lots of boys spit. Some of the real gross-outs even had spitting contests out behind the school. And he hadn't actually been looking at her when he did it. Then he slowly raised his head, and it was like those smouldering eyes of his were equipped with bayonets that pierced her. After a moment he turned and went back into the house, slamming the door loudly behind him, or letting it slam.

Cally could feel herself blushing. As she turned and walked back to her chaise, she glanced at her own house, at Mr. Curran, standing at the window now, looking over at the place where the boy had been standing.

At least she had some space of her own. A smile crept across Carolyn's face as she stood in the middle of the third-floor room and twirled slowly around. Wait until Cally and Luce saw this place! It was the most fantabulous room a person could ever want.

Halfway down the second-floor hallway in Greatgran's house was a door. The door led onto a staircase. And the staircase led up to a room whose ceiling sloped on two sides, an enormous room that occupied the whole top of the house. It had windows on three sides, looking out over the front of the house and the back of it, and onto the roof of the house next door. Each window had been hung with brand-new, pale-blue floral curtains; a matching bedspread lay on the brass-framed double bed that was now her own. She had her old chest of drawers and desk and chair, and two sets of bookcases all in the room, and still there was enough floor space to have a twelve-person slumber party. The place was at least three times bigger than her bedroom back at the apartment. Plus, because she was way up on the third floor and Greatgran was way down on the first, her mother hadn't put too many restrictions on her radio-playing. "Just so the neighbours don't complain," was all she had said.

She flopped down onto the bed and sighed. Maybe this wasn't going to be *quite* so bad as she had thought. Probably it wouldn't exactly be a picnic either. Greatgran wasn't the easiest person in the world to live with. Besides the fact that she clearly didn't like Carolyn, Greatgran also scared her. The thing was, you never really knew what was going on inside Greatgran's head.

But it wasn't as if she had to be *with* Greatgran all the time. Only for meals. And at that, only two meals a day once school started. And maybe her mother would let her bring her breakfast upstairs to eat while she got dressed in the morning. She smiled as she peered around the room again. Then her eyes strayed out the front window.

God, it was him! Mark Simons. Her heart pounded in her chest. He was so incredibly handsome, she didn't care what Luce said. Pete Willets was okay, if you liked the brawny jock type. But Mark Simons was something special. For one thing, he wasn't a loudmouth like Pete. He didn't always have a gang of people hanging around him.

Mark was a loner. She'd heard kids say that he liked to read a lot, and that he was interested in being a writer. Usually when she saw him in the hallways, he was threading his way through the crowds with his nose in a book, using some bat-like kind of radar to keep him from smashing into people and lockers. He almost never looked up. But when he did, and when he saw her, he always smiled. Shyly. Of course, he'd never actually said anything to her. But there was something about the way he looked at her when he smiled that made her think he was the most wonderful guy in the whole world. She would give just about anything if he would actually notice her long enough to decide he liked what he saw, and to ask her out.

Now there he was, loping down the street in front of her house. She wondered what he was doing in the neighbourhood.

"Carolyn!" her mother called from somewhere below. "Carolyn, I need you."

Carolyn groaned. Not now, Mom, she muttered under her breath. She wanted to watch Mark, to see where he was going.

"Carolyn, can you hear me?"

"Yeah, Mom."

Mark was slowing down. He stopped to pat the head of the dog next door, then let the dog lick his hand.

"Right now, Carolyn!"

Rats. Reluctantly she pulled herself away from the window and thudded down the stairs.

"Did ya like the movie?" Pete asked.

"Yeah. Yeah, it was nice."

Sitting there in the dark all that time while Pete gobbled a bucket of popcorn and guzzled a gallon of orange soda, sure, it was terrific. She had on her best dress, she'd done her hair up specially for the occasion, and he sat there like an eating machine, crunching and slurping and not paying the slightest bit of attention to her. Going to the movies with Cally and Carolyn would have been more fun. For sure it would have been less humiliating.

"Yeah," said Pete as they reached the lobby and headed for the exit. "Yeah, it was okay." He held the door open for her, and when they stepped out, she felt the heat and the wetness of the night close in on her cool skin like a steamy washcloth. "You want to go out and grab a bite to eat or something?"

She wanted to disappear off the face of the earth, that's what she wanted to do. Well, thank God Carolyn had been moving today. If she hadn't, Luce would have told her she had a date with Pete at long last. And Carolyn would have been thrilled for her. And then tomorrow morning Carolyn would have called to ask, So, how did it go? How was it? What's he really like? And she would have had to make up some story about how she didn't really like him after all, how he wasn't as nice as she had thought he was going to be, how you couldn't judge a book by its cover. That kind of stuff. So that she wouldn't have to tell the real story: namely, that Pete had turned out to be not very interested in her. He hadn't even touched her, for crying out loud. Not once. He hadn't even slipped an arm sort of accidentally on purpose around her shoulder. Or dropped a hand onto her knee.

"Luce?"

"Huh?" She stared up at him.

27

"I said, you want to go out for a bite to eat or something? You hungry?"

She shook her head slowly. The longer the evening lasted, the more complete her humiliation would be and the more unbearable her pain. She wanted it to be over with, quickly, like a slice of the sword blade through the neck. A clean stroke.

Pete nodded. "I'll walk you home," he said.

She wasn't surprised when he didn't take her hand in his, or slide an arm around her waist, when he just loped along beside her, gazing up at the stars and, every so often, over at her.

When they reached the sidewalk in front of her house, she stopped first. He walked on another pace and a half, turned, looked quizzically at her, then slapped his forehead with the palm of his hand.

"This is your place, right?" he said. "Dumb me! I walked right by, thinking I was on my way to my house."

Would it never end? Now he was telling her her company was so darned scintillating he had forgotten she was even there.

He peered into her eyes with those grey storm clouds of his. "Hey, you okay?"

Sure, she was fine. Only if he said another word about it she was going to burst into tears. Maybe even if he didn't. She could feel her lower lip quivering and when she told it to stop, it didn't listen. She started to turn away, but he caught her by the arm and pulled her back. "I said, you okay?" he repeated, his voice raspy, as usual, but gentle besides.

She nodded. Once she was staring into his eyes, she couldn't make herself look away again. Then he was standing up close to her, so the ends of their noses were almost touching, and he was looking at her in such a strange way that she couldn't imagine what he was seeing.

Then he kissed her. He wrapped his arms around her and pressed her so close to him that she could feel every muscle, every bulge, every hollow, and he kissed her.

"I'll call you," he said when he finally pulled away from her. Then he strode up the street, getting smaller and smaller in the darkness.

I could die, thought Luce. Right this very minute, I could die and I'd be the happiest dead person in the world.

She thought the scream had come from a nightmare. She was less sure about the sound of shattering glass. The latter sound had come when she was already sitting up in bed, her heart pounding, her pulse racing, her mouth dry, staring in terror into the darkness, the scream still echoing in her ears, and focusing at last on a wall and a room she didn't recognize.

Then there were more sounds. Real sounds. Familiar sounds. Like her mother's voice. Except she couldn't recall the last time she had heard her mother shouting hysterically, "Carolyn, Carolyn, come quickly, I need you!" Then a dog barked, just like in the movies when there's a disturbance in the middle of the night. The dog convinced Carolyn that the breaking glass had been real. She swung her legs over the edge of the bed and ran.

There was no one on the second floor of the house, where her mother's bedroom was. Carolyn ran down to the ground floor. "Mom!" she called. "Mom, where are you?"

"Out here!" came a distant voice from somewhere at the back of the house. As she raced through the kitchen, Carolyn saw where the glass had shattered. The window over the kitchen sink was now more or less *in* the kitchen sink. Carolyn ran through to the back door and flung it open, stepping out onto the back porch. Way down at the bottom of the yard she could see two shadowy figures, one in a flowing white robe, chasing after the first, but cautiously, picking its way along as though less sure of its footing. Carolyn bounded down the steps. Then, astonishingly, the first figure disappeared. The second stopped dead. So did Carolyn.

"Mom?" Her voice was as thin as a thread, tentative.

"Carolyn, where did she go?"

"Who?"

"Go get the flashlight," her mother called.

"Where is it?"

"I don't know," her mother called in exasperation. "It must be in one of those boxes."

Then a beam of light danced into the yard. Carolyn's mother at the bottom of the lawn, and Carolyn, at the bottom of the stairs, both looked towards it. It was coming from the property next door and illuminated a gap in the heavy hedge that separated the two yards. Through it came the figure in flowing robes. Carolyn strained into the darkness. The robed figure was Greatgran, and she was being guided by a man in pyjamas and a robe. He had his arm around Greatgran and was steering her towards the house. Behind them came a third figure. Carolyn blinked when she first saw it. Please, she begged, let me be dreaming this. Let this all be some weird nightmare. Mark Simons stepped into the yard behind the man and Greatgran.

"Mrs. Quaid?" said the man. Carolyn's mother hurried over to him and took Greatgran by the arm. "I'm Jason Simons," the man said. "This is my son, Mark. We live here, next door. We heard the commotion and when I went out to investigate, I found Mrs. Harding here in our yard." He smiled pleasantly at Greatgran, as if her nocturnal visit were no inconvenience whatsoever. "Just thought I'd bring her back safe and sound," he said.

"Thank you," said Carolyn's mother. Even though Carolyn couldn't see her face, she could tell by the tone of voice that her mother was embarrassed.

"Another thing," said Mr. Simons in his pleasant voice. "I thought I heard some glass breaking . . . "

"The kitchen window, I'm afraid," said Carolyn's mother.

"Would you like me to take a look at it?"

"Oh, no, I'm sure it'll keep until morning."

"I'll send my son over to measure the window in the morning," said Mr. Simons.

"Oh, that won't be necessary . . . "

"Nonsense," said Mr. Simons. "Three ladies living alone." He smiled at each of them in turn, Greatgran and Carolyn and Carolyn's mother. "It's the least we can do, right, son?"

Mark Simons nodded. He didn't say a word.

3

It was something Cally thought she would never forget. It was so weird, it was funny. At least it would have been funny under different circumstances. Each and every kid who walked into homeroom that first day did exactly the same thing.

Usually on the first day of school everybody walked in chattering away and there'd be so much noise the teacher would have to threaten detentions to get a lid on it. It was the same thing in every single class the first day of school because everyone was getting reacquainted with everyone else and comparing timetables and summer vacations. Usually it took a day or two before everybody settled down to work.

But this first day was different. At least it was in Cally's homeroom. You could hear the noise out in the hall. And when the faces would first appear in the doorway, the mouths would be flapping away. Kids talking. Then the minute they crossed that threshold and did what everyone always did first time into a new class, check out who was there, their mouths would clamp shut and their eyes would pop open. And they'd all be staring at the same thing. Or, rather, the same person.

His name was Orlando Verdad. Cally found that out

from when the teacher called roll. That had been good for a laugh too. Cally's homeroom teacher this year was Mr. Carlisle, who taught history. He was a plump old guy with a pot belly, a quadruple chin, thick glasses and a lisp. The kids all called him Fudd, after Elmer Fudd in the Bugs Bunny cartoons. Fudd didn't seem to like kids. He didn't seem to like teaching much either. What he did was, he stood up at the front of the class, his big butt pointed directly at them, and he copied out stuff from the history text. Almost word for word, Cally had discovered. And he expected them all to be quiet and copy down what he wrote, so that by exam time they would have it all memorized and could shoot it back at him when he asked for it. Fudd hardly ever looked at the kids. And homeroom was no different.

He bowled into the room, head down, like he was trying to make the most of aerodynamics, and slapped his attendance book down onto his desk. Then he slapped his butt down onto the chair. He flipped the book open and without even looking up, began to read the roll, last name first, first name last. Underhill, John; Usher, Patricia; Venn, James; Verdad, Orlando.

Underhill, John, said "Present" in a bored voice, like he wished he wasn't. Usher, Patricia, said "Here" with no discernible inflection. Venn, James, said "Yeah." Verdad, Orlando, said nothing. That was when Fudd looked up. He opened his mouth as if he was going to say the name again. Then his eyes landed on Verdad, Orlando, and his mouth sagged open and all four chins got compressed into his chest and everyone started to laugh. Everyone except Verdad, Orlando.

"Well, I'll be a monkey's uncle," said Jeff Troy. "We got a nigger in school."

"Nah, you're not the monkey's uncle," Pete said lazily. He had his arm draped around Luce as he leaned against the wall beside the cafeteria entrance. "*He's* the monkey's uncle." Everyone laughed.

"Where'd he come from?" Bob Everett asked. "I didn't think they let niggers live around here."

"Where did *you* come from?" said Luce. "Better yet, where do you think you are? Alabama, before the Civil War? We're in 1964 here, Bob. Get real."

Bob turned red in the face. He scowled at Luce.

"I don't think that's what Bob meant, Luce," said Pete.

"Well, what did he mean?"

"I think he meant that niggers don't live around here. And so he's naturally surprised to see one pop up in our school." He was saying it all in a fake-serious tone of voice, and the guys around him were snickering.

"He meant that he doesn't think the guy belongs here," Luce said sullenly.

The one thing about Pete was, he was a real tease. He was always putting her on in front of his friends, letting them all get a good laugh at her expense.

"Well, of course he doesn't belong here," said Pete. "If he belonged here, don't you think there'd be more of them around? But there aren't, are there? He's the only one. I bet he's going to find it a lot harder here than he thought."

Luce frowned. "What's that supposed to mean?"

"Never you mind, Luce," Pete said. He pulled her closer to him and kissed her on the lips right in front of everybody. He seemed to like to do that, and she couldn't decide how she felt about it. Sometimes it made her feel really special because he did it and he didn't care who saw; it was like he was proud of her or something. He kept telling her how beautiful she was, and he was always trying to get his arm around her and touch her, feel here and there. But, on the other hand, well, it was weird how the rest of the guys looked at her when Pete did that, and it made her shiver sometimes, wondering what they really thought about her.

"I'll see you later, hon," Pete said, releasing her, giving her a little pat on the bum.

"I thought we were going to have lunch together," Luce complained.

"Uh-uh," said Pete, shaking his head slowly. "I got practice."

"Now? It's the first day of school!"

"I didn't get to be the star of the basketball team by eating lunch," said Pete. "See you later, babe." And before she could offer any further protest, he was gone, swaggering along with his gang, as if she were the furthest thing from his mind.

She sighed and peeked into the cafeteria. Carolyn was in there with Cally. She wished Carolyn was alone, so she could talk to her. *Really* talk to her. But no. Good old Cally was always around. Jeeze, it was pathetic how that girl clung to Carolyn. You'd think she would have died without her.

Cally smiled up at Luce as Luce pulled out a chair to join them, but Luce didn't believe for one minute that she was being sincere. Maybe she fooled other people with that perennial dopey smile of hers, but she didn't fool Luce. No way. And when she said "Where's Pete?" as if it were the most innocent of questions, Luce really wanted to smack her one.

36

"Practice," said Luce. She glanced at Carolyn, who looked like she hadn't slept in a decade. She was pale and thin looking. "What's the matter with you? You look like death warmed over."

"It's her Greatgran," said Cally. "She's messing up Carolyn's life."

"Yeah, well, you have my sympathy," said Luce as she slumped back in her chair. "Old people are a real drag. Not to mention they're kind of disgusting to be around. My Grandpa Davies . . . "

"Please," said Cally sharply. "I'm trying to eat here."

Luce arched an eyebrow and fixed Cally with a piercing look. "Really?" she said, casting her eyes up and down Cally's body. "I would have thought you'd be frantically dieting. Skirts are getting shorter this year, Cally, dear, and let's face it, your thighs aren't getting any slimmer."

"We can't all hobble along on little toothpicks like you," snapped Cally.

"Jealous."

"Never! You look like something from a concentration camp."

Luce stuck out her tongue, then glanced at Carolyn. "You're being awfully quiet," she said. "What's the matter?"

"Remember Mark Simons?" said Cally. "Well, he . . . "

Luce swivelled her head around slowly until she had Cally in full view. Then, in a slow, dry voice, she said, "I asked Carolyn. I didn't ask you."

Cally made a sour face, but she shut right up, the way she always did unless Carolyn jumped in on her side. But right now Carolyn didn't seem to be listening to a word they were saying.

"Carolyn . . . " said Luce.

"It's Mark." Carolyn's chin was resting in her hands; her elbows were propped up on the table; her face looked kind of mashed. Remind me not to sit like that around Pete, Luce thought. It's extremely unflattering.

"What about Mark?"

"He lives next door to Greatgran."

Luce rolled her eyes. For someone who took home A-studded report cards, Carolyn could be so stupid. "Carolyn," Luce said patiently, "that's good, not bad. When the guy you're interested in lives next door, it's perfect. You have instant access to him, night or day."

"He's a person," said Cally. "Not a drive-in restaurant."

"What a shame," said Luce. "And what a shame you're not a banana, Cal. If you were, then you could split."

"Very funny."

"Thanks, guys," muttered Carolyn. "My life is crumbling, and all you two can do is bicker. Thanks one heck of a lot."

"I still don't get the problem," said Luce.

Carolyn shook her head. "What's not to get? The guy lives right next to my great-grandmother. He and his dad have caught her wandering around their yard twice now and have had to bring her home. He knows she's ga-ga."

"Your Greatgran's mental state isn't exactly a secret," said Luce. "It's not like you haven't been broadcasting it to everyone for years . . . "

"But I *like* him!" Carolyn cried in exasperation.

"So? You think he thinks insanity is hereditary? Or that if he kisses you, he's going to catch it? Or maybe you're really thinking ahead, to marriage and having crazy babies? Is that it?"

Carolyn's eyes narrowed to slits, like gun battlements, from which she could fire.

38

"You don't get it," she said, her teeth clenched, each word laboriously formed.

"I guess not," said Luce. "I mean, you *could* look at it this way: he knows the worst about your family. You've got nothing to hide."

"I know," said Carolyn glumly. "I know."

Why me? thought Cally. Two thousand kids in the school, five hundred of them in her grade, and probably half of those enrolled in biology. Why, out of all those kids, did it have to be her? And why did those odds never pan out in her favour when it was something she desperately wanted, like to lose fifteen pounds, all of it off her thighs and bum, in time for summer?

She couldn't tell what the worst part of it all was either. When Mr. Brewer started reading out the list, dividing the whole class into pairs, lab partners, that same eerie hush that she had noted in homeroom fell over the biology class. People started sneaking peeks at Orlando, who, again, had chosen the seat way in back of the room, farthest from the door. And she could see that each time a kid's name was called as the first name in a pair, that kid tensed up, waiting to see if the next name would be Verdad, Orlando.

If Cally noticed it, then probably Orlando did too. She turned her head just a little so she could look at him out of the corner of her eye. He was just sitting there, hands clasped on his desktop, eyes straight ahead, staring at the corner of the blackboard or one of the coloured diagrams of the human body on the wall. Like he didn't care.

Then she heard her own name. "Wright, Cally." Her body became rigid. She didn't dare look at anyone while she waited. "Verdad, Orlando." The air came leaking out of her. She felt faint. She could see kids staring at her, most of them relieved, a few looking sorry for her, another couple thinking it was funny. Orlando didn't move or flinch.

"Okay," said Mr. Brewer. "You've got your partners. Now you're going to get your assignments. Teams one, two, three and four," he said, "I want you to go out and each pair find twelve different species of vegetation."

"Now?" someone from team two asked.

"In a minute," said Mr. Brewer. "After I've handed out all the assignments. Okay. Teams five to eight, twelve different forms of insect life."

"Does each team have to find twelve kinds different from the kinds any of the other teams looking for the same thing has found?" someone else asked.

Mr. Brewer shook his head, as if he had just come out of the water and was trying to clear it. "I bet you can't say that fast five times in a row," he said. Most of the class laughed. Orlando didn't. "The short answer is, no. But each team does have to find twelve. Okay. Teams nine through twelve. Twelve different specimens from twelve different mammals. Notice I said twelve different *specimens*, people, not twelve different mammals. I don't want to be deluged with cats and dogs and bunnies tomorrow. Just specimens from them, bits of hair, saliva . . . "

"Yuck!" said one of the girls.

"What are we going to do with all this stuff?" someone else asked.

"We will proceed with lesson one tomorrow," said Mr. Brewer. "The microscope and the preparation of slides. Okay, away you go. And, people? Treat this assignment seriously, will you? It's not an excuse to play hookey."

While everyone else got up and flooded out of the room, Cally remained at her desk and peeked over at Orlando. He was motionless. He doesn't like me, she thought. He doesn't seem to like anybody. And he's not even trying. But, God, she was stuck with him as a lab partner for the whole year. No way she was going to flunk biology just because she got him for a partner.

She sucked in a deep breath, pushed her chair away from her desk and marched right over to him. When he didn't look up, she cleared her throat and said, "Excuse me. I'm Cally Wright. I'm your lab partner."

When he looked up at her, his eyes were dark and cold and hard. Like lumps of coal. "So?" he said.

"So," she said, "I guess we'd better go and do our assignment, huh? I mean, I'd hate to get the year off to a bad start." She rushed the words out; he made her feel so nervous, like he wished she'd just go away.

"Oh, yeah, I'd hate to see you get the year off to a bad start," he said in a snotty voice.

"Well, then, we should get going."

"Suppose you get going," he said. "You find six specimens. I'll find six. Simple, right?" He was looking at her like he thought *she* was simple, an idiot.

"But . . ."

He stood up, unfolding himself from the chair, and she realized for the first time how tall he was. And while her mouth hung open and she tried to think of something appropriate to say, he strode right out of the room.

4

"*A*re you sure you can manage?" Elizabeth Quaid asked.

"Yes, I'm sure I can manage," said Carolyn. She hadn't been entirely sure at first, but the more times her mother asked the question, and the more times she repeated the statement, the more she thought, how bad can it be? Her mother and her grandmother were only leaving for the afternoon. They would be back in time for dinner. What could possibly go wrong?

"We're going now, dear," Grandma Dell was saying to Greatgran. "Carolyn will be here if you need anything."

"Who's Carolyn?" Greatgran asked petulantly. Her lip twisted down like a child pouting because it can't get its own way.

"Carolyn, your great-granddaughter," Grandma Dell said a little irritably. "Right there." She pointed a long finger at Carolyn.

Greatgran peered over at her. Carolyn stood on the other side of the room and smiled back. Behind her smile, she was angry. Greatgran had no trouble at all remembering who Grandma Dell and Carolyn's mother were. But she never remembered Carolyn. Lately Carolyn found herself being reintroduced to her great-grandmother almost on a daily basis. And every time Carolyn came into the room or sat down at the table, Greatgran gave her a peculiar look and retreated into herself. She almost never talked to Carolyn.

"She doesn't like me," Carolyn had complained to her mother.

"She's just not used to you, that's all," her mother said.

"She hates me."

"She does *not* hate you. She just can't always remember who you are, that's all."

"If she liked me, she'd remember."

Greatgran was staring at her now. Then she cupped a hand around her nearly toothless mouth and said in a loud whisper to Grandma Dell, "She looks like Kathleen."

"She doesn't look like anyone at all except who she is," Grandma Dell said with annoyance. "Really, Mother, I just finished telling you. This is Carolyn."

"Who's Kathleen?" asked Carolyn.

Carolyn's mother shrugged.

"No one," Grandma Dell said sharply. She pulled on a pair of black gloves. "We have to go now. You be good, Mother, and don't give Carolyn any trouble."

"Carolyn?" Greatgran said foggily.

Grandma Dell rolled her eyes. "I left the number on the kitchen table, child," she said to Carolyn. "If anything happens, just call us. We can be home in twenty minutes."

Carolyn nodded.

"I know what you mean," said Clarissa Burns. "I mean, it's not as if they actually *do* anything. In fact, they really keep to themselves, don't they?"

Cally's mother sipped her tea from a mug, peering over the rim at her neighbour from across the street. Her eyes darted to Cally, who was standing at the counter, peeling potatoes for supper.

"And there are actually only three of them," said Clarissa. "The boy must be at least Cally's age . . . "

"He's in several of Cally's classes," said Mrs. Wright.

Mrs. Burns arched her eyebrows as she glanced at Cally. "Is he now? I bet that's interesting, isn't it, Cally? What have you been able to find out about him?"

Been able to find out about him? She made it sound like an assignment for James Bond.

"Cally?" said Mrs. Wright. "Mrs. Burns is talking to you."

"I don't know anything about him," said Cally as she hacked at the potatoes. God, some of these women had nothing to do all day except stick their noses into other people's business. Talk, talk, talk. Why did her mother put up with them?

"But he *is* your lab partner," said Mrs. Wright.

"Is he now?" said Mrs. Burns. Her voice was getting higher and squeakier each time she said it. "Now, that *is* interesting. Where's he from, Cally?"

"I don't know."

"Didn't he tell you?"

Cally scowled down at the potatoes. If she scowled directly at Mrs. Burns, her mother would give her hell later. Manners. Manners are very important. They're practically the most important thing in the world, the way most adults act.

"He doesn't say much," said Cally. And did she ever understand why not, the way most people acted around him. They either stared at him, right out in the open, or

45

ignored him, like he was invisible, or gave him a hard time, like he wasn't welcome. After that first time, that thing with Pete, Cally had thought getting the business had to be the worst part of it all. But now she wasn't so sure. Because he didn't always get the business. But he always got stared at, and he always got ignored. And he was always alone.

"Does he get along okay with the other kids?" Mrs. Burns asked, trying to sound innocent, like a lost little lamb. But there was a sharp look in her eyes, like a face in a picture Cally had seen once, a scene from a public hanging, with a lady standing at the bottom of the gallows, staring up at the body suspended from the rope, a hungry look in her eyes.

"He gets along," Cally said impatiently. "Mom, I've finished with this. Can I go now?"

Her mother frowned and for a minute Cally thought she was going to say no. But Mrs. Wright just nodded. Cally ran out of the house into the yard. It was a cool fall day; the leaves were changing on the trees, some of them were drifting down into the yard. She gazed next door, into the Verdads' yard, and watched the maple leaves drift earthward there too. She never saw the parents. Well, almost never. Mr. Verdad had some kind of job downtown. He'd come out of the house every morning at precisely seven-thirty. He always had on a suit and tie, and his shoes always had a high polish on them. He carried a briefcase and, these dark fall days, usually had an umbrella furled under his arm. He walked all the way up to the top of the street, crossed the highway, and stood at the station on the tracks with so many of the other fathers, waiting for the train into the city. But, unlike a lot of the other fathers, he always walked alone.

She had seen Mrs. Verdad only twice since the day she had moved in. Once it was a Sunday morning, and Mrs. Verdad wore a pale-pink dress with a frilly, flowery pink hat and she got into the car and drove away. She was probably going to church, Cally thought. Another time she had seen Orlando's mother standing on the porch, hanging the wash out on the line.

She saw Orlando daily. Besides being in her homeroom, he was in her biology class, her history class and her English class. He always sat at the back. He never volunteered any answers, but if called upon, he would usually deliver the correct answer in a slow, quiet voice that carried the bite of anger. He never smiled. He never answered any of the jeers that kids hurled at him. When Pete went so far as to trip him in the cafeteria, sending him facefirst into a hot chicken sandwich slathered in gravy and mashed potatoes, he just picked himself up and walked away.

It was probably because of this detached, aloof, don't-give-a-damn attitude that everyone was floored when he actually showed up to try out for the basketball team. Luce had kind of summed it up when she had said, in her ever-brassy voice, from the stands, "I don't effing believe it."

But there he'd been, standing tall and black in the middle of the court, waiting for someone to tell him what to do. And the coach was kind of looking at him with this gleam in his eyes. Coach Deacon was from the States. New Jersey. Pete had told Luce who had told Carolyn and Cally that Coach Deacon's New Jersey teams had been practically all black. And even Pete had begrudgingly said, "Yeah, well, athletics seems to be one thing they do right."

"And music," Cally had put in.

Pete had snorted in contempt. "Their music sucks," he sneered. "Give me Elvis every time."

"Elvis?" Luce had said, and had given him a playful punch in the elbow. "Haven't you heard, Pete, there's been a British invasion. It's the Stones now, and the Beatles, and the . . . "

But when Orlando showed up for try-outs, Pete looked even less enthusiastic about the athletic prowess of black people. He also didn't look too happy about the shape of Orlando's body, which, besides being taller than Pete's, was leaner, better toned, a less flashy kind of look. Kind of like Sean Connery as James Bond, thought Cally. With one obvious difference. And she couldn't help wondering, did Orlando have a girlfriend? Couldn't. There weren't any black girls in school, and she had never seen any around his house. But maybe he used to have one wherever he lived before. And if he did, maybe he missed her and maybe that didn't help him in a place like this.

"Cally?" It was Carolyn nudging her. Giving her a funny look. And Luce was staring at her too, giving her the same strange look. Cally's cheeks burst into flame.

"What?" she said. "What's the matter?"

Carolyn leaned over and pressed her mouth to Cally's ear. "You're practically drooling," she whispered. "And I'm not the only person who noticed."

Cally had been so embarrassed she thought she was going to die. But she couldn't get up and walk away. If she did that, everyone would know that she knew they had been watching. She looked down at the toes of her sneakers and breathed a heavy sigh of relief when the try-outs started and everyone's attention shifted back to the action on the gym floor.

She thought the coach was going to kiss Orlando or something. The guy was great on the floor. He had moves that dazzled even Pete. He could control the ball, and make it dance, and turn from everywhere on the court and kind of chuck it up into the air, and it would arc beautifully on its way to the basket, then, *schwump*, right through and plunk onto the floor underneath. He never missed. Not once. And even Pete missed now and again.

When it was all over, when the last whistle shrilled, Coach Deacon went over and slapped Orlando on the back and told him, great job. Everyone else just stared. Pete glowered. The rest she heard from Luce.

When they hit the showers, the guys all just stood there in their sweaty clothes. Stood around and stared at Orlando, who was getting undressed.

"I mean, can you *imagine?*" said Luce. The way her eyes were glistening, it seemed to Cally that if anyone *could* imagine, it would be Luce. "They're all standing around watching the poor jerk strip down. And you know that guy, eh, he never looks at anyone. He just goes about his business as if he's the only effing person left on the face of the earth . . . "

"People don't exactly make it easy for him," Cally had said.

"Yeah, well, maybe if the guy didn't walk around with his flat little nose in the air like he thought he was so superior to everyone else, things would go better for him." She stuck her tongue out at Cally, then turned to Carolyn. "So, anyway, he's getting stripped and no one else is, and when he turns around to go to the showers, he finds out he's the only person in the whole effing place who's naked. And then, because he's so proud, you know, he never shows any emotion, it'd probably kill him, he's

49

stuck. He can't get dressed again without having his shower. That would be admitting defeat. So he walks to the shower and gets in it and he has to take that shower while all the guys are standing around staring at him. I mean, can you *imagine?*"

"I think that's disgusting," said Carolyn.

Cally felt like hugging her.

"Oh, for Pete's sake, it was just a joke," Luce said. "The guy asks for it, after all. It's not like he makes any attempt to be friends with anybody . . . "

"How do you suppose most people would act if he did?" said Cally.

"Well, we'll never know, will we?" said Luce in her snottiest voice. "Because he thinks he's King Shit around here and he's never going to try."

"What about you?" said Cally. "Or Pete? If Pete was nice to him, it could make things a whole lot easier."

Luce exploded with laughter. "Get real!" she said between convulsions of mirth. "Pete? Friendly to that guy? He doesn't even want to play on the same team as him."

"Well, he hasn't got much choice unless he quits the team," said Cally. "I saw the posting this morning. Orlando made first string. Right up there with Pete."

Luce's smile died. "Pete won't like that," she said.

"Who cares?" said Cally. She swept the remains of her lunch off the cafeteria table and hurled it into the garbage.

Now, as she stood in the back yard, shivering a little – the air was colder than she had expected and she had left the house without a jacket – it seemed to her that every time Orlando's name came up in conversation, she ended up walking out of some place. She peered over at the

Verdad house and wondered if Orlando was inside, and, if he was, what he was doing.

"She's way too sensitive," said Luce. She had her legs draped over the arm of one of the living-room chairs. The radio was cranked up as loud as Carolyn would permit on the main floor of the house. It wasn't all that loud. Carolyn was in the kitchen, preparing lunch for Greatgran, while Luce pored over the top fifty songs of the week, trying to work as many titles as possible into a little story. The radio station was giving away free albums every day; all you had to do to win was make dumb stories out of song titles. Luce did it faithfully every week. She spent more time on it than she spent on her homework, but so far she hadn't won a thing. Carolyn helped her out now and again, but the idea of having it announced over the radio to the whole city that Carolyn Quaid had been stupid enough to waste four hours composing a ridiculous story for the sake of a Dave Clark Five album made her uncomfortable; she always told Luce not to bother putting her name on the stories.

"I think she has a point," said Carolyn as she opened a can of soup and dumped it into a saucepan. "Pete should leave the guy alone."

Luce rolled her eyes. "Jeeze, don't tell me you're going to take her side on this one."

"It's not an exclusive, Luce," Carolyn said. "I mean, she didn't make up her position, you know. There are plenty of people in this world who happen to agree with her."

"Yeah, yeah, yeah," said Luce with complete disinterest, and that bugged Carolyn too. When Luce was win-

51

ning an argument, she never let up. But when she was losing, she'd let loose with one giant yawn and then she'd change the subject and would never go back no matter what you said. "Hey, you want to walk down to the village with me this afternoon? I need a new pair of shoes. My mom gave me some money."

Carolyn plunked the saucepan onto the front burner of the stove and turned the heat on high. "I can't go anywhere until my mom and my grandma come back," she said. "I told you that already."

"Okay, okay," Luce said petulantly. "Jeeze, some people are pretty irritable today, not that I'm going to name names."

"That'll be a first," muttered Carolyn under her breath.

"What?" said Luce. "Did you say something? I didn't hear you."

"Nothing," Carolyn sang out.

While the soup started to simmer, she hunted out a tray from the cupboard above the sink and laid a place mat upon it. Then she got a soup bowl and a soup spoon and put them down onto the tray. She put the kettle on to boil and dropped a tea bag into the two-cup pot Greatgran had used for decades.

"Greatgran," Carolyn called when the kettle started to boil. "Greatgran, time for lunch."

Luce appeared in the kitchen, sniffing the air. "What is that?" she asked, her nose wrinkled in distaste.

"Cream of mushroom soup."

Luce came a little closer and peeked into the saucepan. "Yuck, gross," she said. "I hate that stuff. Cream of anything is always gross, especially when it comes out of a can."

Carolyn shrugged. "Greatgran likes it," she said. "And

it's easy for her to eat. You don't need teeth to eat soup."

Luce screwed up her face even tighter. "Gross, gross and double gross," she said.

Carolyn got a ladle from the drawer and ladled a generous portion of soup into the bowl on the tray.

"She's not going to eat out here?" Luce said.

Carolyn shook her head. "She hasn't been feeling well the past couple of days. Mom said I should let her eat in her room. She's got this recliner she likes to sit in . . . "

"Spare me the details," said Luce, drifting over to the fridge and opening it, peering inside. "I only have one set of grandparents left, thank God, and they live out west. I hardly ever see them."

"Lucky you," said Carolyn, piling the sarcasm on so high that even Luce couldn't miss it.

"Well, you're the one who's always complaining about her," said Luce. "So don't act as if it's all my idea."

Carolyn said nothing. After all, it was true what Luce said. Carolyn complained about Greatgran all the time. She picked up the tray and carried it out of the kitchen to the back of the house where the den used to be, where Greatgran's bedroom was now, with a bathroom right off it, so she didn't have to climb up any stairs for anything.

"Greatgran, it's lunch time," said Carolyn in a sing-song voice. "Luce, you want to get the door for me?"

Luce backed out of the fridge, chewing on a cold chicken drumstick. She sauntered down the hall to where Carolyn was, twisted the doorknob and swung the door open. Carolyn entered the room.

"Hiya, Greatgran," she said with a cheeriness she didn't feel. It was hard to feel cheery around Greatgran, especially when she gave you a pretty fair imitation of the evil eye.

Greatgran was dozing in her recliner. When Carolyn called her name for the third time, her eyes drifted open. When they fixed on Carolyn, the old lady jumped.

"Kathleen," she breathed. Her face went white, her jaw went slack. "Sweet Jesus in heaven, it's Kathleen."

Carolyn approached the old lady cautiously. Who *was* this Kathleen person? "I brought you your lunch, Greatgran. It's me. Carolyn."

Greatgran was smiling. She reached out with one hand to touch Carolyn, but Carolyn backed away.

"Kathleen," murmured Greatgran. She seemed wide awake now. "Kathleen, is it really you?"

Carolyn took another step back towards the door. "Greatgran, it's me," she said, her voice loud with fear. "It's Carolyn."

Greatgran's beatific smile faded. She peered through narrowed eyes at Carolyn, then fumbled for her glasses on the small table beside her recliner. Her fingers were stiff, but she managed to get them to the bridge of her nose. She stared again at Carolyn.

"Who are you?" she demanded.

Carolyn fought the urge to turn and run. It scared her when Greatgran acted like this. Temporary amnesia, her mother called it. Old age, Grandma Dell said. Whatever it was, it was spooky.

"Greatgran, it's Carolyn. Your great-granddaughter."

"Get out of here!" the old lady shrieked.

"But, Greatgran . . . "

"Get out! Get out! Get out!" She was struggling so hard to escape from her recliner that Carolyn was terrified she was going to hurt herself.

"Jeeze," said Luce, sticking her head through the open door. "What's going on in here?"

"Get out! Get out! Get out!"

Carolyn started backing away from the frenzied old woman.

"Get out! Get out! Get out!"

"Holy eff!" said Luce. "Her eyes look like they're going to pop out of her head. She gonna have a stroke or something?"

"We'd better call someone," said Carolyn. "The number's on the kitchen table. That's where they are."

"You want *me* to call?"

"Yes!"

"Jeeze, what do I tell them? Your great-grandmother is freaking out? You want me to tell them that?"

The doorbell rang.

"I'll get it," yelled Luce, and she was off like a shot, leaving Carolyn at the door, peering in at Greatgran but terrified to approach her. What if she really did have a stroke? Mom and Grandma Dell would come home and there'd be Luce, legs slung over one of Greatgran's best armchairs, bits of cotton wool stuck between her toes, she'd be painting her nails scarlet. And Carolyn would be there, crying, of course, wracked with guilt because somehow this was all her fault. Everything bad that ever happened seemed to be her fault. Greatgran would be stretched out on her recliner, her hands still formed into tight little fists, her tongue hanging out. Well, you see, Mom, I was taking her lunch in and she just kind of freaked right out . . . I *told* you she didn't like me.

"Everything okay in here?" a male voice asked.

What the heck is this? thought Carolyn. Someone up there having a good laugh? All of a sudden I'm the cosmic jester of this lunatic court. I spend practically my whole life dreaming of Mark Simons coming to my door, and the moment he picks to do it is the exact moment Greatgran is screaming at me like I'm the devil. Perfect.

"Oh, Mark," she said as cheerfully as she could manage. "What are you doing here?" She almost melted when she looked at him.

"I heard yelling," he said. "I thought maybe I should investigate. I saw your mom and Mrs. Persimmon going out a little while ago."

Greatgran had stopped shouting, but she was still glowering at Carolyn.

"I was just bringing her her lunch," Carolyn said. "And she said something about Kathleen and started screaming at me."

Mark smiled. "Oh," he said. "I bet she was having a nap when you came in, right?"

"Right," said Carolyn, regarding him with surprise now. "How did you know?"

"It's happened before. My mom used to come over every now and then to see Mrs. Harding, you know, if she was going to the market or into town. She'd stop by here first and see if Mrs. Harding needed anything. And if she'd ever catch her napping, well, sometimes Mrs. Harding would wake up and she'd be all confused and she'd sort of . . . "

" . . . freak out?" suggested Carolyn.

"For want of a better phrase." He looked over and smiled at Mrs. Harding. "If you think about it a while, you can just imagine how scary it would be if you suddenly couldn't remember where you were when you woke up, or if you had trouble putting names to faces, that kind of stuff. You just have to be patient. And stay calm." He looked down at the tray Carolyn was carrying. "That food still hot?"

Carolyn nodded.

"I'll take it then," he said, and he gently pried the tray from her hands and carried it over to the old woman. "Hi, Mrs. Harding," he said politely as he set the tray down onto the little table beside the recliner. "Remember me? Mark Simons from next door."

Mrs. Harding studied him a moment, then her face relaxed into a smile. "The boy who rakes the leaves," she said.

"That's right," said Mark. "You hungry?" He pulled up a chair close to the recliner and sat down to keep her company while she ate.

Carolyn watched from the doorway, too afraid to go back in, too fascinated to pull away.

"How come you're so good at that?" she asked him later, after he had carried the tray back to the kitchen.

"So good at what?"

"And modest too," said Luce jokingly from the doorway. "I just love a man who's modest."

Carolyn shot her a dirty look. Couldn't Luce see that she was finally with the man of her dreams? A friend who was really a friend would leave a person alone under those circumstances.

"So good with my great-grandmother," Carolyn said at last.

Mark shrugged. "I don't know. I like her, I guess. And I sort of understand her. My grandfather lived with us for the year before he died, and he was in pretty bad shape a lot of the time. At the end, just before they took him to the hospital, he didn't recognize any of us. I always thought that would be the most incredibly awful way to die, all alone because there isn't a soul on earth you recognize, not even your own family."

"You never hear a stalk of celery complain," said Luce. "Or a head of lettuce, for that matter."

Mark stiffened. His whole demeanor changed. "Well, I guess you girls have everything under control now," he said. "I'd better get going."

Carolyn opened her mouth to say no, don't go. Stay. But she could tell he wouldn't want to, and didn't want to embarrass herself any more by asking. She could have killed Luce.

5

"Guess you guys are getting all excited about the big game, eh?" said Luce. She had been hanging around in the hallway outside the gym, waiting for basketball practice to end. She didn't mind going to the games. But she could live without practice. During practice the whole gym stank of sweat and there weren't any other mitigating odours to take that pukey edge off it. Now Pete was out. His hair was still wet from the shower, and he plunked a hand on the back of her neck and used it to drag her closer, so he could kiss her.

"Pete," she murmured, embarrassed. The rest of the guys were coming out of the locker room now, and they were all staring, some of them making smart-ass noises.

"What's the matter?" said Pete in a loud voice so everyone could hear. "You don't like to be kissed?" Some of the guys snickered.

Luce turned scarlet. She pulled away from Pete a little. "So," she said, "you want to do something now?"

"Honey, I always want to do something with you," said Pete. He slipped an arm around her again and pulled her back to him. "How about you and me go get a bite to eat, okay?"

"Okay."

The door to the locker room swung open again. This time Orlando came out. He walked without looking at the people around him; he held his head high. All the guys grew silent when they saw him. Their eyes followed him down the hallway, and they were still fixed in the distance after he had turned the corner and disappeared from sight.

Luce looked at Pete. Something in the hard greyness of his eyes made her shiver. "Come on, Pete," she said, tugging on his arm. "Let's get out of here."

"You are going to the game?" Luce asked again.

Cally had to count to ten and back down to one again very, very slowly to prevent herself from slugging Luce right in the nose.

"Yes," she said. "I'm going to the game. Why? Is there some reason I shouldn't go?"

"No," said Luce. "No reason at all. Except that you don't know the first thing about basketball. You don't even like basketball." She peeked around Cally to Carolyn and flashed a wicked smile. "This wouldn't have anything to do with a certain outstanding player, would it, Cally Wright?" she asked.

"Outstanding?"

"By virtue of his colour at least," said Luce.

"Luce . . . " That's all Carolyn said whenever Luce started up. Just Luce, in a kindergarten-teacher tone of voice, as if that was going to stop Luce from saying whatever stupid thing she had to say.

"Well, you've got to admit," said Luce, "he does kind of stick out like a sore thumb. Although the reverse would be true if there were ever a power failure. No one would be able to find him."

"That's it!" said Cally. She gathered up her lunch, carried it across the cafeteria to the nearest vacant seat, and plunked down into it. When she glanced over at the two of them, she could see Carolyn giving Luce the eye, then Carolyn getting up and walking slowly over to where Cally was now sitting.

"She doesn't mean half of what she says," Carolyn said as she slid into the seat opposite Cally.

"It's the other half, the half she does mean, that really gets to me," Cally said. "She'd be right at home in Mississippi or Georgia or some place like that."

Carolyn didn't say anything. She just fiddled with a corner of Cally's lunch bag, twisting it up and then untwisting it again. "You still going to come to the game with us?" she said after a little while.

Cally opened her mouth to say no. Just about the last person on earth she wanted to spend an evening with was Luce. But if she did say no, then she'd have to go to the game alone. Either that or stay home. Neither option appealed to her very much.

"I'll go if she promises to keep her big mouth shut about him," she said at last.

Carolyn smiled, sort of.

"Even if she promises," she pointed out, "that doesn't necessarily mean she'll stick to it. Luce is one of the only people I know who breaks all her New Year's resolutions before Christmas time. You just have to put up with her, that's all."

Cally sighed. The fact was, Carolyn was right. Cally either put up with Luce along with just about everybody else, or she put up with loneliness. Some choice.

61

"Yeah," she muttered. "I guess you're right."

"Great," said Carolyn. "Listen, you be at my place at seven and we'll swing by Luce's and pick her up. Okay?"

"Okay."

The gym was packed. Luce had told Carolyn maybe twenty times: don't be late. When your team is playing its first game of the season, and when your team was last year's city champion – which Pete had told Luce maybe twenty times — you have to get there early to get a seat.

Carolyn arrived late at Luce's house. She said it was because of Cally, who was dressed like she was going to tea at Buckingham Palace, not to a high school basketball game, for crying out loud. Cally had sort of apologized, but just sort of. "My mom got home late," was what she said. "I couldn't leave Walter at home all alone and I didn't think you'd want me to bring him along." Well, no kidding.

Anyway, by the time they got to school, the gym was packed.

"We're gonna have to stand," Luce grumbled.

Carolyn was peering over at the stands. No imagination required to figure who she was looking for, thought Luce. She took a quick look herself, but Mark Simons wasn't there. But, "Hey, look, I think I see a place!" Luce grabbed Carolyn by the hand and started to drag her to the far end of the stands.

"Hey, Cally!" called Carolyn, and Luce wished she hadn't. Cally was busy staring around, probably looking for that Orlando guy. What bugged Luce wasn't just the fact that Cally stared at him all the time; lots of people did that. You could hardly help yourself, the guy was so *ob-*

vious. It was also the *way* Cally looked at him. It was downright embarrassing. Even Pete had noticed and he had started ribbing Luce about it: "What's the matter with your friend? She got the hots for Sambo?" So far Pete hadn't actually said anything in front of Cally, so there hadn't been major trouble. But if Cally didn't smarten up soon and pull herself together, there *would* be trouble, Luce could practically guarantee it.

Cally stumbled towards them, and Luce led the way to a few feet of vacant bench in the third row. She trod on several feet to get there, and when she plunked her butt down, the kid beside her, a mousey brunette, said, "Hey, that's saved!"

"Tough," said Luce as she shoved her hips over hard, muscling the kid, pushing her a little more to the side to make room for Carolyn and Cally.

Carolyn seemed upset. One thing she didn't like was trouble. Any kind of trouble. Big trouble, little trouble. A kid complaining fell into the category of trouble for Carolyn. For Luce it was just a pain in the ass. And there was Carolyn, standing, biting her lower lip, saying, "Well, it *is* saved."

"It's not saved anymore," snapped Luce. "Now it's taken. First come, first served. That's how it works."

"Well . . . "

"For crying out loud, Carolyn, plant your ass. The game is going to start any minute."

Carolyn was getting red in the face, which was perfect. Luce had said everything loudly on purpose. Because she knew if she did, she'd embarrass Carolyn. And she knew Carolyn well enough to know that when Carolyn was embarrassed, her immediate reaction was to make herself as small a target as possible for the ridicule of others.

Carolyn dropped onto the vacant bit of bench without another word, and Cally slid in beside her.

"Gee," said Cally, gazing around, "I had no idea basketball was so popular."

"Where have you *been* all your life?" said Luce.

"Same place you've been," Carolyn said acidly. "You didn't know a thing about basketball until you started lusting after Pete."

"That's not true!" Luce sniffed indignantly. She hated it when Carolyn did that, made her look stupid in front of Cally. Cally was the one who didn't know anything. But Carolyn was always defending her, always telling Luce to go easy on her, treat her nicely. A person could puke. Who did Carolyn think she was anyway? A candidate for sainthood?

A roar went up when the teams burst into the gym. Luce was on her feet, shouting, calling Pete's name, smiling proudly and waving to him as he spotted her and nodded at her. That's *my* boyfriend, she thought. The rest of you chicks can eat dirt. *I* scored the best player on the whole team.

Pete nodded at her. He even flashed her a smile. But a peculiar smile. Like maybe his mind was elsewhere. Which it probably was. It *was* the first game of the season. A big deal.

Luce sneaked a peek at Cally. Lord, she was doing it again. Staring at the black kid. Luce shook her head in disgust. Some people had no pride.

The game got off to a good start. At least it seemed to Luce to be a good start. Pete scored two baskets right off. How much better could it be? But, despite that, Luce noticed a funny tension in the stands. People had their eyes glued to the action on the floor. But that was normal for any basketball game, right? Only, after a while, people stopped cheering and rooting; instead, they were nudging each other and whispering.

"Is there something going on?" Luce finally whispered in Carolyn's ear. She felt dumb having to ask, especially after what she had said to Cally. But another thing about Carolyn was, if you asked her a question straight out, she answered you straight out. She never gave you one of those dumb-bunny looks. She never acted like you were stupid if you had to ask.

Carolyn kept her eyes on the court. "Watch Pete," she said to Luce through grim, taut lips. "And watch Orlando."

Luce was baffled. But she watched for the next minute or two, and it became obvious, even to her. Orlando would be in the clear, he'd be alone with no one on him. But no one would throw him the ball. His own teammates just let him move around the court all on his own. The only time he got the ball was when he took it away from the other team. Luce stared mutely at Carolyn as Coach Deacon signalled for time out.

"They're freezing him out," Carolyn murmured, like she couldn't believe it.

The coach was talking to Pete now. And where the coach was red in the face and scowling, Pete was just standing there, smiling faintly, looking sort of baffled, shrugging. When the game started again, nothing changed. In fact, it got worse. The opposing team seemed to click to what was happening, and they more or less stopped trying to guard Orlando. It was getting quieter and quieter in the stands. Luce couldn't take her eyes off Pete.

Coach Deacon flagged time out again. He started

65

across the floor towards Pete. Orlando got there first, taking long strides, not like he was in a hurry, but just striding purposefully over to Pete. He stood in front of Pete, taller than him by maybe an inch and a half, then suddenly, so quickly Luce hadn't even seen it coming, he punched Pete right in the belly, using both hands clasped together as a kind of weapon. Pete doubled over and dropped to his knees. Then all hell broke loose.

"Did you see what he did? He attacked Pete!" Luce was on her feet again. "That stupid nigger attacked Pete!"

"Pete had it coming to him," snarled Cally with a viciousness and a conviction that stunned Luce. She stared open-mouthed at Cally for a moment before pushing her way out of the stands and wading through the melee on the floor to get to Pete.

The two coaches and the referee were trying to pull everyone off Orlando. It took a while. Then the announcement: the game was forfeited. A howl went up from the crowd.

"Pete? Pete, you okay?"

He was down on his knees on the hard gym floor, still clutching his belly. But when he lifted his head to look up at her, he managed a smile. A victory smile, it seemed to Luce.

"Cally! Cally, where are you going?"

Cally didn't stop. She saw them pull all the guys off Orlando. She saw the coach lead him over to the door to the locker room, and she saw Orlando first resist, then break free. Orlando took off out the side door of the gym. Cally ran after him.

He was striding down the hallway towards the nearest

exit, his fists still clenched at his sides. Cally opened her mouth to call to him, but the name didn't come out. She knew he wouldn't stop even if she did call him. He was going to walk out into the chilly night in his basketball uniform. He'd catch his death.

He shoved open the exit door, which was bouncing off the outer brick wall and swinging closed again by the time Cally reached him. She ran the last few steps, then fell into stride beside him. If he noticed her, he gave no sign. He kept his eyes straight ahead.

They were clearing the school yard before she found the courage to say, "Orlando?"

No answer.

"Orlando, I'm really sorry about what happened."

Wham!

He stopped. He turned. He looked down at her with those blazing dark eyes of his. "Why?" he said, his voice as hard as his muscles. "Did you know it was going to happen? Maybe you helped plan it."

Cally was stunned. All she could do was stare helplessly up at him. He stared stonily down at her, then he dismissed her with his eyes and started to turn away.

"You don't really think I'd be involved in something like that, do you?" she said when she managed to find her voice.

His back was to her. She was as inconsequential to him as a mosquito, and about as pesky. But it wasn't fair what he had said.

Finally, he turned. His mouth was twisted into a kind of sneer, the closest thing to a smile she had seen on him.

"I didn't have anything to do with it," she whispered, not afraid of what he might do, but of what he thought of her.

"Why should I believe you?" he said in his deep voice. "Why should I believe any of you?"

Cally glanced around. Then she faced him again. "There is nobody else," she said. "There's just the two of us."

"Just me and my lab partner," he said. "Well, honey, this isn't biology class. Why don't you just run back to your little friends and leave me alone?"

Cally thought about it. She thought about Luce screaming how "that nigger" had hit Pete. She thought about the whole team, the guys who were supposed to be on the same side as Orlando, first shutting him out, then crashing all over him, his own team trying to hurt him. Carolyn too, just standing there, not understanding where Cally was going, and probably not approving. And she suddenly felt very alone.

"I don't want to go back there," she said quietly.

There was a flash of genuine curiosity in his eyes. But only a flash, less than the time it takes for a fork of lightning to illuminate the sky. Then he said, "Suit yourself," and walked away into the night.

6

"*I* don't effing believe it," said Luce. "That guy throws the first punch, and they suspend Pete from the team. I mean, that takes real brains."

"Orlando got suspended too," Carolyn pointed out as patiently as possible. But her patience was wearing thin. She had been listening to this same lament all day; they were at Carolyn's locker now, collecting Carolyn's books for the weekend.

"Big deal," muttered Luce. "His suspension is only half as long as Pete's."

"None of this would have happened if Pete hadn't started it."

"Pete's been playing basketball for years and he's never ever been suspended," Luce pouted.

"Does the expression, there's a first time for everything, mean anything to you?" said Carolyn.

Luce rolled her eyes. "Spare me," she said. "Besides, you know perfectly well that none of this would have happened if it hadn't been for *him*."

"Him?" Carolyn arched her eyebrows and slammed her locker shut. "The guy does have a name, you know."

"Yeah. Pretty dumb one, if you ask me. Orlando's a place in Florida, for crying out loud, not a person's name."

Carolyn shook her head slowly.

"What?" demanded Luce. "What did I say now?"

"You never cease to amaze me, Luce. What on earth makes you think that the place Orlando wasn't named after a person Orlando? I mean, America was named after some guy."

"Was not," said Luce irritably.

"Was too."

"Get real."

"*You* get to the library and check it out. The guy's name was Amerigo Vespucci. He was a navigator or something."

"Big deal."

"And, anyway, maybe where Orlando comes from, his name is ordinary. Like Pete or Joe or Bill."

"Would you stop with the lecture!" Luce snapped. "You're giving me a headache. Besides, I'm still right. If Orlando had never come here, none of this would have happened."

Why do I suddenly feel like pulling all the hair out of my head, Carolyn thought. Why does she always do this to me?

"Luce, you could say the same thing about Pete. If he had never come here . . . "

"Don't be ridiculous," said Luce. "Pete was born here." She was digging around in her purse now, and finally pulled out a compact, which she snapped open. "So," she said as she checked her makeup, "you want to walk me over to Pete's?"

Which reminded Carolyn. "Where is Mr. Team-Spirit today anyway?"

Luce pulled out some lipstick and spread it on her lips. Then she fussed with her hair. "His mother freaked when he came home last night," she said, clicking the compact shut and shoving it back into her purse. "So did his dad. They made him stay home from school today to rest."

"Oh." It was the only safe thing Carolyn could think of to say.

Cally paused a moment and leaned on her rake. She had done about half the yard. An enormous pile of yellow, red, orange and brown maple and oak leaves was heaped near the very back. But the way Walter and his little pal Ben were leaping in and out of it, it didn't look as though the stack would stay neat for very long. Cally didn't care. When she had been Walter's age, she had spent hours playing in the leaves in autumn. She loved their brilliant colours, the way the brown ones crumbled to dust in her hands, the leafy-smokey smell in the air as people burned them in incinerators.

As she leaned on her rake, resting, she felt inside her pocket for the piece of notepaper on which she had carefully copied down the weekend homework assignments for the classes she had with Orlando. Her idea had been to march right up to his front door and hand it to him and maybe get the chance to talk to him again. But even if he didn't want to talk, maybe he would get the idea. And she wanted desperately for him to get the idea, to see that she *was* different, that she really *was* sorry for what had happened to him. She was certain she was the only kid in the school to think of making sure he got his homework, even if she sure wasn't the only one to remark on his absence.

Of course she hadn't marched right up to his front door

after school. Instead, she had done what she always did – she had chickened out. She kept thinking about the way he had looked at her, the way he had assumed the worst. He thought she was just like everyone else, just like the Petes and the Luces of the world.

Damn it!

She flung the rake down, squared her shoulders and headed for the front of the Verdad house. Her stomach started churning the moment she circled around the edge of the low cedar hedge. Her knees turned to water when she actually put the first foot down on the Verdad lawn. She could hear her heart thumping inside her chest; her mouth was dry, and for one horrible moment she thought, I'm going to throw up all over their porch. But she refused to allow herself to do anything like that.

She climbed the steps. There were six. They seemed more like sixty. And when she got to the top, time seemed to slow almost to a stop. The time between when she pushed the buzzer and when she heard footsteps was an eternity. She thought that would give her the chance to prepare herself. But when Orlando yanked the door open and scowled at her, her mind went completely blank.

Orlando stared at her through the screen door.

She stared back. She had an almost insane desire to laugh; this was like that silly kids' game, staring and staring to see who will blink first. But she didn't laugh. He would almost certainly have misunderstood if she had. Nor did she talk. Let him go first this time.

"What do you want?" he said at last, giving the word a brush stroke of contempt, disdain.

She calmly reached into her jacket pocket and pulled out the paper. He didn't open the door to take it. Instead, he said, "What's that?"

"I copied down the homework assignments for biology, English and history," she said. "You know, since you weren't at school today."

"I have them already," he said.

Cally couldn't hide her feelings any longer. Her shoulders slumped. "Oh," she said, and didn't care if he heard the disappointment or saw the tremble in her lips. Let him get a good laugh if he wanted. "Sorry to have bothered you then," she murmured. Now to get off his porch and back into her own yard without heaping more humiliation on herself. She turned.

"The principal was here this morning," he said unexpectedly. And, as she turned back, "And the vice-principal and the coach and some lady from the school board. They were all here."

God, what should she say? What was she *supposed* to say?

"Those guys, they're falling all over each other apologizing," he said, and laughed bitterly. Cally nodded. He stared at her so long and so hard she could feel her cheeks burn. "You're the only kid who's said anything about it," he said.

She smiled. He *did* see. He could tell. She wasn't like the rest of them, not at all.

"You want to go out with me?" he said. He kind of snapped the words out at her. It wasn't at all the way she had imagined it would be when a guy asked a girl out. "Tomorrow night. I'm going to a party."

"Oh, sure," she said. "Yeah."

"Will your mother let you go downtown? We can take the bus."

"I'll ask her," said Cally.

"You do that," he said. "You let me know."

73

She didn't feel the grass beneath her feet as she walked over to her own yard. She didn't feel anything at all, except a vague sense of unease, a kind of dread.

There was music coming from the back of the house when Carolyn got home. Strange music. Not top forty stuff. Not the Beatles. Not Elvis. It sounded kind of like, well, she wasn't quite sure what it sounded like.

"Irish folk music," her mother said without looking up from the books and papers she had spread out all over the dining-room table.

"Irish folk music?" Carolyn shook her head. There was no accounting for some people's taste. "You actually *like* that stuff?"

"It's not so bad," her mother said with a shrug. "I like Sinatra better. Or Andy Williams."

Carolyn rolled her eyes. Her mother was *so* old-fashioned.

"It's not my record," Mrs. Quaid said. "That nice boy next door brought it over for Greatgran."

"Mark?" Carolyn couldn't believe it. "Mark was *here?*"

"Still is, I think," said her mother with a twinkle in her eyes.

Carolyn threw her arms around her mother and gave her a kiss on the cheek. "Thanks, Mom," she said before running out of the room.

"Don't thank me," Mrs. Quaid called after her. "It wasn't my idea."

Carolyn raced through the kitchen and down the back hall. The door to Greatgran's room was open. A record player Carolyn didn't recognize had been set up on one of Greatgran's tables, and a record was spinning on it. In the middle of the floor, Greatgran, holding Mark, was dancing. Her face was radiant. Carolyn had never seen her so happy.

It was a moment before Mark looked over the top of Greatgran's head and saw Carolyn hovering in the doorway. He smiled.

"Come on in," he said. "Join the party."

Carolyn grinned back. "Best invitation I've had all day," she said as she stepped across the threshold.

As Greatgran swirled around in Mark's arms, her eyes lit on Carolyn and the smile faded from her face. She jumped backward, as if scared, knocking the record player and sending the needle squealing across the record. The silence that followed lasted only a moment. Then Greatgran screamed at her, "Now see what you've done! You've ruined everything! Everything!"

Carolyn backed up, then turned and fled down the hall, through the kitchen, up two flights of stairs to her room. She flung herself down onto the bed, started to count slowly under her breath, and wished she were old enough to live on her own. Seven . . . eight . . . She could hear a little tap on her bedroom door, then the sound of the knob being twisted . . . Nine . . . ten . . .

"Carolyn?"

Her mother pushed the door open and stepped into the room.

"Carolyn, what's the matter?"

Carolyn glowered at her mother. How could she stand there and pretend she didn't know? Hadn't Carolyn told her dozens of times?

Her mother sighed and came over to sit on the edge of the bed.

"It's Greatgran, isn't it?"

"She hates me," Carolyn sobbed. "Ever since we moved in here, she doesn't want me around."

"I know," her mother said quietly. "And I'm sorry."

Carolyn's tears stopped flowing. She sat up and stared at her mother. "You know?"

"I'm not blind." Her mother reached over and brushed Carolyn's hair from her eyes. "At first I thought it was just the change. Greatgran's been alone in this old house for a long time now. I thought she was just having trouble getting used to us."

"But she used to like me," Carolyn said. "I mean, she was *nice* to me at least." She certainly never screamed at me and treated me like some kind of leper, she thought.

"Greatgran is sick, Carolyn. Her mind doesn't work the way it should. She can't always remember things, and what she does remember isn't always clear."

"But she doesn't treat you the way she treats me."

Mrs. Quaid sighed. "I know," she said. She studied Carolyn a moment. Carolyn held her breath. Whenever her mother looked at her like that, she was thinking of the best way to tell Carolyn something. And usually it was something bad. "Carolyn, I think you should make more of an effort with Greatgran."

"I'm trying," Carolyn protested. "It's hard to make an effort with someone who freaks every time you walk into the room."

"Maybe you give up too easily," said Mrs. Quaid. "You know, you could learn a thing or two from that Simons boy . . ."

"Mark. His name is Mark," Carolyn said irritably.

What was it? All of a sudden nobody could call people by their names.

"Mark gets along well with Greatgran. His mother tells me he has a real empathy for elderly people."

"Empathy?" What the hell was that?

"Empathy. The ability to share another person's feelings or ideas. He seemed to *understand*. And he's very patient. Maybe he could give you some pointers."

Carolyn hurled herself off the bed. "What am I supposed to do? Go down there and admit to him that my own great-grandmother freaks out every time she sees me?"

"I hardly think that would be news to him, dear. *He's* not blind either."

Great! Just terrific! Carolyn flew down both flights of stairs and almost collided with Mark at the bottom.

"Oh, there you are," he said. "I was wondering where everyone had gone. I have to go now . . . "

"Go, go!" she said. "Go! I don't care!"

Then she turned and ran out of the house, leaving him standing there.

"Where exactly is this party?" asked Mrs. Wright.

"Downtown."

"Downtown isn't a very precise location, Cally. Do you think you could narrow it down for me a little?"

Cally picked up a plate from the dish drainer and began to dry it.

"Gee, Mom, I'm not sure exactly. But he said it was downtown. We're going to take the bus."

"The bus?" Mrs. Wright glanced sharply at her daughter.

"Come on, Mom. I can go, can't I?"

"I don't know, Cally." Her mother rinsed a glass and set it into the drainer. "I hardly know the boy."

77

"You don't know him at all," said Cally. "They've been living next door for nearly two months . . . "

"Six weeks."

"Six weeks, two months, whatever. I bet you've never said a word to his parents."

"I've never even *seen* them," her mother said quickly. Little red splotches appeared on her cheeks.

"You could have gone and knocked on their door and introduced yourself," said Cally.

"They could have done the same thing."

Cally sighed impatiently. "It's not the same, and you know it."

"Watch that tone of voice, young lady. This is your mother you're talking to."

"Sorry," Cally muttered. She dried the rest of the plates in silence. Then, as she started on the glasses, she said, "I want to go to the party with him, Mom. It's important."

"I don't think it's a very good idea."

"But he asked me."

"If he asked you to jump off a cliff, I suppose you'd be begging me to let you do it."

"Mom . . . "

"No, Cally. I don't want you to go, and that's that."

Cally dried a glass as she studied her mother. Then, very quietly, very calmly, she said, "I bet you'd let me go if he was white."

"Colour has nothing to do with it," her mother said so quickly, so automatically, that Cally felt as if she had just pulled the string on one of those Chatty Cathy talking dolls they advertised on television.

"If you don't want me to go, I guess there's nothing I can do about it, Mom," she said angrily. "But do me a big

78

favour, okay? Don't lie to me about why you don't want me to go with him. Don't pretend colour has nothing to do with it. Colour has everything to do with it, and you know it."

She flung the dish towel down onto the counter and glowered at her mother. This time she wasn't going to run out of the room all upset. This time she was going to stay, she was going to fight this thing out.

Her mother continued her washing, slamming soapy cutlery down into the dish drainer, knife, fork, spoon, *plunk, plunk, plunk.*

"Mom?"

When her mother turned, there were tears in her eyes. "Mom?"

"Have you thought about how hard it could be for you, going out with a boy like that? Have you thought about what people will say?"

Cally sighed. Good old Mom, always thinking about others, even if it was mostly about what others would say.

"I already know, Mom. Jeeze, the poor guy's had a rough time at school. He has no friends. Everybody steers clear of him. It's not right."

"But why does it have to be you?" her mother cried. "Of all the girls in that school. Of all the boys . . . "

"Mom, I just want to go to a party with him. I'm not going to marry him or anything. At least not yet."

Through her tears, her mother managed a feeble smile. Then she nodded.

"Pete? Pete, you down here?"

It was dark in the basement. She'd tried the switch at

the top of the stairs, but nothing had happened. She had had to feel her way cautiously, inching her hand along the bannister, kicking out with her feet.

"Straight to the bottom, then a sharp right," Pete's mother had said before scurrying into the living room with a bowl of popcorn.

"Pete?"

She got to the bottom and turned. At the back of the house she could see the pale, flickering light of a TV set. He was probably in the rec room.

"Pete?"

She trod cautiously, her arms feeling out the empty air all around her, like a blind person, her feet shuffling forward on the hard tile floor.

"Come on, Pete, turn a light on, will you?" Pete and his stupid games. Like, did he really think a little darkness was going to scare her? "Pete?" Okay, so maybe she was just a *little* scared. After all, lots of people kept all kinds of junk in their basements; she could trip over an old tire or a length of pipe and break her neck.

From out of the pitch blackness, something, someone grabbed her.

She screamed.

It laughed. *He* laughed.

"Pete, you bastard!" She was really mad now. She hated being scared like that, and hated it even worse when some pervert thought it was funny.

"I love it when you talk dirty," he said. He still had his arms around her and was kissing her now. She hated that too. Not the kissing, but the way she always melted when his lips touched hers. The way she knew he knew he could do practically anything to make her mad; then to make her forgive him, all he had to do was kiss her.

80

"Pete," she murmured, "can't you put on a light?"

He kissed her again, pressed her up so close she could practically feel his heart beating against her chest. Or was that her heart? Then he pulled her gently through the darkness. Something snapped. A small lamp illuminated one corner of the room.

"Sit down," he said, sinking onto the sofa. "I was just watching a movie."

She dropped down beside him. "How are you feeling? You okay?"

He shrugged. "Better," he said. "Now that you're here."

She crossed her fingers and hoped the mood would last after she had told him what she had come to tell him.

He draped an arm over her shoulder and let his hand hang down kind of accidentally over her breast. It made her tingle all over.

"Did you hear anything from school today?" she asked.

"You mean about what happened?"

She nodded.

"Yeah. The pricks suspended me for it. Can you beat that? I just organize myself a little non-violent protest, you know, like little old what's-his-name over in India . . . " He snapped his fingers while he struggled to recall what's-his-name's name.

"Gandhi?"

"Yeah. Him. I mean, I'm out there on the court. I'm making my point in a totally non-violent way, when, *whammo*, a guy decks me and it's suspension city. Him, hell, he deserved it. But me?" He shook his head.

"It sure wasn't fair that he got only half the suspension you did," said Luce sympathetically. She was relieved that he knew all about it, and she was surprised that he was taking it so well.

81

Pete's hand whipped back off her shoulder.

"What did you say?" He was mad now. Really mad.

"I said, it wasn't fair he only got half the suspension you did," Luce repeated, pulling back from him a little, terrified of the burning in his eyes. "I thought you knew. I thought . . ."

"Let me get this straight." Pete was up now, padding in front of the sofa in his bare feet. "Just let me understand this. That little jungle bunny decks me one out there in front of maybe two hundred witnesses, and he gets away with less time than me. Is that what you're telling me? I've got to sit out twice as many games as that god-damned . . ."

"Pete, please, calm down." She got up and went to him, tried to put her arms around him. He pushed her. "Get away from me!"

"But, Pete . . ."

"Get away from me. I need some room. I need to think."

She crept back to the sofa and crouched in one corner, staring at the image on the TV screen, while Pete paced up and down, up and down.

As Cally disembarked from the bus, she wondered why she had bothered to argue with her mother to be allowed to come. Certainly Orlando had managed to contain his emotions when she had told him the answer was yes.

"Well, I'll be down at the bus stop at seven-thirty," he said. "Meet me there." Period. End of sentence. End of paragraph. End, in fact, of all communication.

She had ignored her mother's raised eyebrows as she left the house alone and made her way down to the end of the street where the bus stopped.

"Hi," she had said shyly, looking up at him, wondering if she had dressed appropriately. He had never really said what kind of party it was, and she had been afraid to ask his advice on the matter.

He looked at her. Then his eyes skipped down to her feet and dragged their way back up very slowly, calves, knees, thighs, going over her, no expression on his face, no way to tell what he thought, until he reached her eyes again and said, "Yeah, hi."

They stood beside the telephone pole that doubled as the bus stop, staring down the road towards the village from where the bus was coming. After a while she stole another glance at him and said, "Is it something special?"

He stared at her as if he hadn't the faintest idea what she was talking about. She felt her face turn scarlet and was glad it was already dark outside.

"The party," she said. "Is it a birthday party or anything like that?"

"It's just a party," he said.

"Oh."

She peered down the road again, and when she saw the headlights of the bus rounding the corner, she didn't know whether to feel relieved or even more nervous. On the one hand, she wouldn't be stuck out on the sidewalk with him, trying desperately to find the right thing to say to him. On the other hand, she'd be stuck with him on the bus, the two of them seated side by side for an excruciatingly long forty-five minutes.

Orlando didn't bother with ladies first. He climbed onto the bus ahead of her, proceeded down the aisle, and took the window seat without even asking her if she might like it. Then he stared resolutely out the window. Once she glanced in that direction and found his eyes in

the window, peering at her. They shifted away immediately.

"Well," she said after the bus had deposited them on
yet another sidewalk downtown, on Sherbrooke Street
West. "So, here we are."

"We gotta take another bus." He said it as if she should
have known.

They waited in silence. The bus, when it came, was a
crowded city bus. They stood near the back and hung on
for dear life whenever the driver negotiated a corner.
Finally, after what seemed like forever, Orlando reached
over to the window and jerked the cord.

"Are we there yet?" Cally asked as she joined him on
the pavement.

"Up there," he said, nodding, and she had to scramble
to keep up with his long, loping strides as he climbed the
inclined sidewalk to a low-rise apartment building. Instead of climbing the stairs once they got inside, Orlando
led her down into the basement. She could hear the pul-
sating music even before he shoved the door open.

She followed him down the basement hallway and
stood back a little as he knocked on the door. When it
swung open, spilling music and laughter into the damp-
ish corridor, Cally saw Orlando do something she had
never seen him do before. He smiled. Fully, radiantly,
genuinely. He stepped inside the apartment. Only when
the guy at the door tapped him on the shoulder and
nodded at Cally did he turn back to her.

"Oh, yeah," he said, his face hard again. "Well, you
coming or not?"

She blushed to her roots and scurried in after him. As
the door swung shut behind her, she suddenly froze.

The room was overflowing with people roughly her

age, all of them now staring at her. She tried to smile, but her lips trembled so badly she finally gave up. She was the only white person in the whole place.

She looked around for Orlando, but he wasn't there, not in the living room anyway. She remained against the door, as if she had been fitted with a coat hanger and hung there. After a few minutes everyone went back to what they had been doing, talking, dancing.

I feel like a fool, thought Cally, standing here like a statue. She eased into the room, trying harder to smile, to make the impression that she wasn't afraid.

There was an empty space on one end of the sofa, and she headed for it. Beside her, two girls were talking. They stopped to look at her, then went back to their conversation. Cally clasped her hands in her lap and forced her body to sway gently in time with the music. Try to look like you're having fun, she told herself. She wished that Orlando would come back so at least there would be someone she knew.

"Hi."

A girl in a short red dress and red shoes was staring down at her, smiling.

"Hi."

"I'm Carlene," said the girl. "Orlando's cousin." She glanced around the room. "This is my party."

"Oh," said Cally. "Looks like everyone is having a good time."

The girl shrugged and raised one eyebrow slightly. "Orlando goes to your school, right?" she asked. And Cally thought, what a funny way to put it, as if it somehow belonged to her.

"We're in a couple of classes together," she said.

"He still hate it?"

85

The question startled Cally, but the girl was peering at her, expecting an answer. "Well," Cally said finally, "I honestly don't know."

The girl shrugged. "Yeah, well, I'd hate it if I was him. Must be awful." She glanced around the room, her body moving with the beat. "I gotta circulate," she said. "See ya later."

"Yeah," Cally said brightly, casually. She almost felt like crying when Carlene left, threading her way among the dancers, smiling, laughing, calling to people. And where *was* Orlando?

She stuck to her little corner of the sofa, glancing at her watch discreetly every now and then. After their initial stares, people seemed to forget about her. An hour dragged by. She thought she saw Orlando over in a corner beside a table of food. But by the time she got to her feet, he was gone. She worked her way over in that direction anyway, thinking maybe she would find him.

She discovered him in the kitchen, perched up on one of the counters, drinking soda from a bottle and talking to some guys. She almost didn't recognize him with that big smile on his face, all the tension and tautness gone, actually having a good time. And that made her angry. He had invited her to come to a party where she didn't know a soul, and then he had abandoned her. He didn't care what kind of time she was having. She marched over to him. When he didn't look up at her, even after the three guys he was with were staring at her, she gave him a little shove. His eyes blazed as he turned to her.

"What do you want first?" she asked. "The good news or the bad news?"

He stared down at her, unruffled. "Give me the bad news."

"The bad news is that you're a complete jerk and I hate you."

Even she couldn't believe that smiley-faced Cally Wright had said that. Orlando seemed less than impressed. He seemed bored. His friends were watching with a little more interest.

"I can hardly wait to hear the good news," he said slowly.

"The good news," said Cally, "is that I'm leaving."

And she spun around and did just that. Blinded by her tears, she pushed her way out of the kitchen, through the crowd at the food table, past the dancers and out of the apartment, out of the building, out into the street.

She stood on the sidewalk, tears streaming down her face. It came to her then that he wasn't going to run after her. He didn't care if she was there or not.

She shivered and gazed down the street, wondering if she could remember how to get back to the bus, back home. The street was dark and deserted and colder now, and she had no idea where she was; she hadn't been paying any attention as long as she was with Orlando and he knew the way.

Don't panic, she told herself. Just don't panic. Think. Which direction did we come from? There? No, I don't remember passing that letter box. Must be the other way, down there. I'll find a bus stop at the end of the street.

She started walking, her footsteps echoing hollowly on the cement. Then, from behind, someone grabbed her. She screamed as strong black hands spun her around.

Orlando!

And back beyond him, in front of the apartment building, was his cousin Carlene.

"It's not my idea," he said. "Carlene said either I get

you to come back inside or I make sure you get home safely."

"I want to go home," she said, and waved at Carlene. "You can just walk me to the bus. Then you can go back."

"Whatever you want," he said indifferently.

As they walked, Cally smouldered inside. It was wrong what he had done. And of all the people to pick on, why her? She had only been trying to be nice to him.

When they reached the bus stop, she expected him to turn and go back. But he didn't. He stood a little way off, hands stuffed into his pants pockets, a scowl on his face.

"Carlene says you hate it at school," she ventured.

He laughed sharply. "Put it this way, I have as much fun there as you had tonight."

"I'm sorry," she said.

He kicked at a pebble. "It's not your fault," he said grudgingly.

"You make me feel like it is."

He didn't say anything, just kicked at the cement with the toe of his shoe.

"If you hate it so much, why don't you transfer to another school? Maybe the one your friends go to, and your cousin."

He looked up at her, opened his mouth to say something, then clamped it shut again. Then he sighed. "My father won't let me," he said at last. "He says I've got the right to get an education anywhere I want, same as everyone else."

"Sounds to me like he means you've got a right to get an education anywhere *he* wants you to," Cally said slowly.

His eyes widened. He stared at her and then began to laugh softly.

Cally frowned. "I don't get it. Did I say something stupid?"

He shook his head.

"I did, didn't I? I said something incredibly dumb. I should have my tongue amputated."

He was wiping tears of laughter from his eyes. "Really, you didn't say anything dumb. Honest."

She didn't know whether to believe him or not, but she was glad she had made him laugh.

She heard a loud whooshing, whining sound and glanced to her right. The bus. She began to fumble in her purse for some change.

"You don't have to go," he said as the bus pulled over to the curb and the front doors swung open.

"I know," she said quietly. "I better, though." She turned and climbed the steps. As she dropped her fare into the box, she caught a glimpse of him watching her. His eyes stayed with her as she walked towards the rear of the bus. Then, on an impulse, she stepped down onto the rear bus step and the back door swooshed open. Orlando smiled as he reached up to help her down.

7

"**J**esus Christ," snarled Pete, which was one of the reasons Carolyn hated hanging around with Luce when Pete was in the picture. The guy was always snarling about one thing or another. Now it was the renovations going on that seemed to rub him the wrong way. They had climbed all the way to the third floor, only to find their passage blocked by trestles and wet paint signs. "The place was closed down for two months in the summer. You'd think they could get their stupid painting done then." He kicked one of the trestles savagely, then spun around and bounded down the stairs.

"What's eating him?" Carolyn whispered to Luce.

"He's pissed off because Orlando comes off suspension for tomorrow's game," said Luce. "Pete's out till Christmas."

Pete deserves to be suspended for life, Carolyn thought.

"You don't think he's going to try anything at the game, do you?" she asked carefully.

The whole subject of Pete and Orlando was a prickly one between them. Luce had gotten it into her head that Pete had done absolutely nothing wrong, that Orlando had been the aggressor, the assailant. And she was just as

91

angry as Pete that he had been suspended from the team for twice as long as Orlando. "Pete's the star of the team," she complained.

"Look at that," Pete said with disgust when they joined him at the bottom of the stairs. "There's a sight that makes me want to puke." He nodded down the hallway, and Carolyn and Luce followed his gaze. There were a lot of kids down there, hanging around the lockers. It was lunch time. But Carolyn had no trouble at all zeroing in on the specific sight that was causing Pete's digestive system such consternation. Cally and Orlando were sitting on the floor in front of Cally's locker. Orlando's arm was draped around her neck; she was looking at him and smiling.

"Jeeze," said Pete. "I hate the way he walks around here hanging onto her like he owned her." He grabbed Luce by the hand and started to pull her down the hall towards them.

Carolyn rolled her eyes. "Why don't you just lay off, Pete?" she said. "They're not hurting anyone."

"Not hurting anyone?" Pete turned on her, eyes ablaze. Beside him, Luce looked at Carolyn, her eyes pleading: don't get him all riled up.

"He got me benched, didn't he?"

"Suspended," Carolyn said coldly. "And you managed to do that all by yourself. You had no right trying to freeze him out the way you did."

There. She'd said it. Finally. Luce standing there with her chin sagging down to her chest took the edge off the victory a little. Luce was her friend. Carolyn wished that she would wake up and see that what Pete had done was wrong. But, jeeze, whoever said love was blind must have been inspired by Luce. Carolyn wondered if there was anything at all Pete could do that would make Luce break up with him. Or at least disagree with him, for heaven's sake.

Pete took a menacing step towards her.

Carolyn refused to flinch. "What are you gonna do, Pete? Slug me one?"

He snarled at her instead.

"Come on, you guys," Luce said in a whining tone. "We're all friends here. Come on."

Friends? The way Pete was looking at her was the way a wolf looked at its dinner while that dinner was still walking around.

"Excuse me," Carolyn said coolly. "I just remembered. I have to talk to Cally." She turned and began to walk away.

"Carolyn . . ."

"Let her go," Pete growled behind her. "Who the hell needs people like that?"

Luce watched Carolyn stride down the hallway and recede into the distance. "I wish you wouldn't make such a big deal about this," she said to Pete.

"Me? Me make a big deal? Why the hell should I make a big deal out of sitting out half the effing basketball season? Why should I make a big deal if some smart-assed jungle bunny like him takes over *my* team . . ."

"It's not your team."

"It's my team. If it wasn't for me, we wouldn't have finished in first place last year. We never finished in first place before. Ever. Not until I joined the team. You can ask the coach, you think you're so damned smart. Go on, ask him who made the difference last year, who led the team to victory." He gave her a shove, and she landed against a locker, hitting her elbow on the funny bone. Why the hell did they call it that anyway? There wasn't a single funny thing about hitting it, but there was always some comedian around to comment on it, "Hey, isn't that your funny bone? How come you aren't laughing?"

She rubbed her elbow as she pushed herself off the locker, and she glowered at Pete.

"That hurt."

"Stop acting like such a smart-ass."

"You stop."

"Me?"

Luce sighed. He was getting all mad again. She was beginning to think the words, I'm sorry, you're right, weren't in his vocabulary. He'd get all mad and you could do nothing to make him calm down. He'd have to do that on his own. And he did. Sometimes it took him longer than other times. But he always cooled out eventually. But never because he'd thought better of it or realized that maybe he was blowing things out of proportion, or, worst sin of all, because he realized he'd made a mistake. No way. He'd calm down mostly because he would run out of the energy it took to be mad. And if you were smart you wouldn't ever mention whatever it was that had got him all worked up in the first place because if you did he'd just get all worked up again.

"Let's not fight," she said wearily.

"You started it."

She wasn't going to argue with that either. No way. "Let's go get some lunch, okay? I'm hungry."

"Is this a private party or can anyone join in?"

Carolyn's head bobbed up. *Please don't let that voice belong to the face I think it belongs to.*

It does.

Thanks a lot, up there, if there is anyone up there, and she sort of suspected there was because no one had this amount of bad luck purely by accident. It had to be part of some divine plan. She felt like an enormous cardboard donkey people kept trying to stick a tail to.

"Oh, hi, Mark," she said. Which sent one of his eyebrows creeping up his forehead.

"Oh, hi, Mark?" he said. "For the past couple of weeks every time I catch sight of you down a hallway or across the cafeteria, you look away, or, by the time I get to where you were, you aren't there anymore. Accident or design?" He said it in a funny sort of way, like he was an actor playing a goofy, slightly pompous version of Sherlock Holmes. "Not only that," he went on, "but when I stop over to see your great-grandmother, you either suddenly aren't home, even though I've seen you come home with my own eyes, or you're taking naps at peculiar hours of the day. Accident or design?"

"Mark, I . . . " Her cheeks were flaming red. What on earth could she say to him? It was obvious he had figured out she was ducking him. But, Lord, how could she face him? Ever since the day she'd acted like a total jerk about her Greatgran, she'd made a point of steering clear of Mark. At first she had told herself it was because she was mad at him. Who did he think he was anyway, just marching into her house any old time he pleased to visit with her great-grandmother! *Her* great-grandmother, not his. And her own great-grandmother preferred him, Mr.-Expert-with-Old-People. That's what really pissed her off. Let Mark walk into the room, a guy who isn't even related to her, a guy who just happens to be the next-door neighbour, and Greatgran is practically falling all over herself to get to him, to talk to him, even to dance with him. But let Carolyn, her daughter's daughter's daughter, her own flesh and blood, walk into the room, and *wham*, suddenly it's the Twilight Zone. First Greatgran staring weirdly at her, smiling faintly at her. And then yelling and screaming and telling her to get out, like she was an invader from Mars or something.

That's what she told herself at first.

The more time she had to think about it, the more she remembered all the things she had said about her great-grandmother. Like how Greatgran ate, and how her dentures hurt, and how she was ga-ga, making fun of her. And because of her, her friends made fun of Greatgran too. Luce saying how gross old people were. And Cally feeling sorry for her because she had to live with one.

And then there was Mark. No one made him come over to the house. No one was twisting his arm to visit Greatgran. No one told him to buy that Irish folk record for Greatgran and to bring it over and play it and dance with her. He did all those things on his own. He *enjoyed* doing them.

She thought about the word, empathy. The ability to participate in another person's feelings or ideas. And it made her think. What was it like for Greatgran to have teeth that hurt so much she had to take them out and eat pureed carrots? And suppose she noticed Carolyn's little looks of disgust, did they make her feel bad? And what was it like to forget? Was it just not remembering, or was it more like having lost something and going looking for it, always looking for it, and never being able to find it because the fog was getting thicker and thicker?

That's when she stopped avoiding Mark because she was mad at him and started avoiding him because she was so ashamed of herself.

"Mark, I . . . what?" he prompted, smiling down at her.

Why was he doing that? Please don't tell me he's empathizing with *me!*

She slumped against her locker. It was bad enough having these feelings. But to actually have to admit them to him? She couldn't. If he didn't already think she was swamp scum, he would by the time she finished her confession, assuming she did confess.

"Did I do something wrong?" he asked.

"Oh, no!" Please don't let him think that.

"Well, if you don't feel like talking, mind if I do? I've got something to show you. Something that might cheer you up a little."

Cheer her up? "I . . . I gotta meet Cally," she said. "I promised I'd meet her at her locker."

"This will just take a minute," said Mark. "I'll walk you to her locker after."

She couldn't think of any way to say no. Besides, she wasn't all that sure she wanted to say no.

He slid a hand into his jacket pocket and pulled out something that looked like a small, flat box. But when he put it into her hand, she saw that it wasn't a box at all. It was a small, hinged picture frame. It fit into the palm of her hand.

"Go ahead," said Mark with a goofy grin on his face. "Take a look at it."

She frowned at him, then pried the two halves of the

frame apart. When she opened it, she saw two old black-and-white photos. She glanced at the photo on the right, and was so startled by it that she almost dropped the frame. She looked at the photo again, then stared up at Mark, her mouth hanging open.

"But . . . that's impossible," she said in a bare whisper. "It can't be."

"What can't be?"

"It's a picture of me!" She felt a shiver run up her spine. In the picture her hair was long and swept back and up. She looked like a Victorian lady. And to the best of her knowledge, she had never posed for a picture looking like that. Which was what made it so spooky. "It just can't be."

"Don't worry," Mark said with a laugh. "It isn't."

"But . . . "

"Looks a lot like you, though, doesn't it?"

"A *lot* like me? It looks *exactly* like me. I feel like I'm looking in a mirror. Except for the dress and hair."

"What about the other photo?" he asked. "Recognize that one?"

It took a moment before she could tear herself away from the first photo. She stared at the second one. Something in the photo drew her. The eyes. There was something in those eyes . . .

"It's Greatgran," she said at last.

Mark nodded. "I'm impressed. I wasn't sure you'd get it. That's your Greatgran when she was a girl. Pauline O'Donnell she was then. And the other one, that's Kathleen."

Carolyn's eyes widened. "Kathleen?" So this was the Kathleen Greatgran was always mentioning.

She stared at the picture again. It was strange to be

looking at a picture that had been taken maybe seventy years ago, and seeing yourself staring back at you.

"Kathleen O'Donnell."

"O'Donnell? Then she was related to Greatgran."

"They were sisters."

She shook her head slightly. "Sisters? But that's impos . . ." She remembered the first time Greatgran had mentioned Kathleen, shortly after Carolyn and her mother had moved in. Carolyn's mother had looked as confused as Carolyn about who Kathleen was. "If she was Greatgran's sister, why hasn't my mother ever heard of her? And why does Grandma Dell act like she's no one important every time Greatgran mentions her?" She thought a moment. "If Kathleen and Greatgran were sisters, then Kathleen would be Grandma Dell's aunt."

"I'm sure there's a good reason," said Mark. "Maybe you should talk to your grandmother."

"Oh, I should, should I?" She snapped the words at him; she couldn't help it. He was doing it again. Digging himself into her family. Now he was acting like he knew more about them than she did.

"Take it easy," said Mark. "I showed you the picture because I wanted you to understand about your Greatgran. She doesn't remember things too well now. And I think it scares her when she sees you. I think a lot of times she doesn't know who she's looking at, you or her sister Kathleen."

"Did *she* tell you this was her sister?"

Mark nodded.

"What else did she tell you?"

"Nothing," said Mark. "The first time I saw this picture or heard of Kathleen was the other day when she gave me this picture."

Gave *him* the picture.

"How do you even know she's telling the truth?" Carolyn said a little bitingly. "Maybe she's confused about that too."

Mark's eyes narrowed. His smile faded. When he spoke again, there was a chill in his voice. "Look," he said, "I'm just trying to help. I know it's not easy for you, having to live with your Greatgran all of a sudden . . . "

"Who says it's not easy?" What was it with this guy? Where did he get off making assumptions like that?

"You mean you haven't found the adjustment a little difficult? I know when my grandfather came to live with us, at first I . . . "

"I'm not you," she snapped. "And my Greatgran isn't your grandfather. And I don't see any reason why my grandmother would lie to me about this Kathleen person." She recalled it vividly: she had asked Grandma Dell, Who is Kathleen? And Grandma Dell had replied, No one. She had also said that Carolyn didn't look a bit like Kathleen, and that was plainly untrue.

"I didn't say your grandmother had lied," said Mark.

"You insinuated it."

"All I said was, I'm sure your grandmother has her reasons for what she does, and I think you should talk to her. Carolyn, your grandmother knows about Kathleen. Your Greatgran doesn't want her to know about this picture." He held up a hand to silence any interruption on her part. "Your Greatgran gave this to me to have new glass put in. You see there's no glass covering the pictures. Your Greatgran dropped it by mistake, and she wants me to get it fitted for new glass. She was afraid if she asked you or your mother, your grandmother would find out and take it away from her. She told me she's been hiding it for years and if

100

your Grandma Dell found out about it, she'd take it away. Okay? So, I don't see how any of this can make you so angry. And especially not with me!"

Carolyn stared at him. She had never seen him so angry. "I'm going to ask my grandmother about this," she said quietly.

"Don't!" He grabbed her arm urgently and squeezed it. The moment he realized what he was doing, he pulled his hand back. "I'm sorry. But please don't breathe a word of this to your grandmother."

"I want to know why she never mentioned this Kathleen person before," Carolyn said. "A member of my own family, someone I've never even heard of."

"If you ask her about it, you'll have to explain about the picture and then she'll want it . . . "

"But, Mark . . . "

"Carolyn, please. Think about your Greatgran."

She stared into his eyes and sighed. After casting another quick glance at the photo, she snapped the two halves shut and handed it back to him. "Okay, Mark," she said. "You're right. But if I can think of a way to ask Grandma Dell about this without having to mention the photo, I will. I want to know."

He smiled. "I guess that's fair enough." He stuffed the photo back into his pocket. "So, I guess you and Cally had some plans for this afternoon, right?"

She shrugged. "Not really. We just usually walk home together, that's all."

"Well, I was wondering . . . do you think Cally would mind walking home alone just this once?"

Carolyn raised her eyebrows. "Walking home alone? Why? Where am I going to be?"

"I thought you might walk down to the village with

me. We could go to the hardware store and see if they'll cut some glass to fit this frame. Then maybe you'd like to stop at the Black Cat for a little pinball . . . "

Carolyn beamed. Funny, she thought, how a moment like this could sneak up on you. She'd spent maybe three hundred hours in the past month or two looking at Mark from afar, thinking about him, drooling over him. And now, after a fight with him, she was suddenly going out with him.

"I don't think she'll mind. We'll just have to stop by her locker and tell her, okay?"

They detoured around the mess of paint cans and drop sheets on the third floor, and strolled down to Cally's locker.

"No, I don't mind," Cally said when Carolyn explained her plans. Then, when Mark looked away for a second, Cally grinned at Carolyn and winked. "Just let me get my junk out of my locker," she said. "Then I'll walk down with you."

While Cally fiddled with her lock, Carolyn dipped her hand into Mark's pocket. Mark glanced at her. Her hand closed around the picture and she pulled it out and opened it.

Mark smiled. "Kind of gets to you, doesn't it?"

"What gets to you?" asked Cally. She was yanking at her lock, but it wasn't opening.

"You oughta get yourself a new lock," said Carolyn, glancing up from the two photographs. "That thing's probably rusted right through."

"It's just stubborn," said Cally.

"Want me to try?" asked Mark.

Carolyn shook her head. "Brawn doesn't work," she said. "Not on that lock. It's all in the wrist."

"In the wrist?" Mark looked skeptical.

"He doesn't believe me," said Carolyn, grinning at Cally. "Listen, Mark, Cally could yank at that thing all afternoon. Me, I just step right out, one quick flip of the wrist, and presto! Instant open locker."

When Mark still looked doubtful, Cally slid aside to let Carolyn in.

Carolyn had the hinged picture frame open in one hand. Her other hand was wrapped around Cally's lock; she pulled it hard.

"Ta da!" she said triumphantly as the lock came away in her hand. She swung the locker door open.

Then everything went black.

She couldn't breathe. She clamped her mouth shut after the first splash poured into her mouth. Then, when she tried to breathe in through her nose, she choked and gasped. Then she coughed and spluttered and thought she was going to throw up. She was afraid to open her eyes, afraid that she might be permanently blinded if she did.

"Take this," Mark was saying. A piece of fabric was being pressed into her hands; she used it to wipe her face as best she could. Then she tried to open her eyes; they were gummed shut at the lashes. Some of the goo crept into her eyes and they began to sting.

"What is this stuff?" she managed to say at last.

"Paint," Mark said grimly. "Black paint."

"Let's get her into the shower," said Cally.

Carolyn felt hands on each of her elbows. She was being guided down the hallway.

"The janitor's going to love this," muttered Mark.

8

"*F*eeling better?" Mark asked as she came out of the girls' locker room with Cally. Orlando was standing beside him.

Her eyes were burning, her skin was raw from the scrubbing she had subjected it to, and she still looked grey in places. Her clothes had been ruined. She carried them in a heavy paper bag Cally had managed to find in the locker room. She was wearing some sweat pants of Mark's and a pair of his gym socks. Cally had lent her the cardigan she always kept hanging in her locker.

"I can still taste that paint," she said. "And when I breathe, I can smell it. What happened?"

"It was a joke," said Mark. "Funny, huh? They put a can of white paint in Orlando's locker. But they screwed it up. The can got caught on the locker shelf. It didn't tip over."

"They?" said Carolyn.

"Pete," said Orlando.

"Pete and that pack of Neanderthals he hangs out with," said Mark. "I saw them out in the parking lot when I went to get some clothes for you. They were having a fine old chuckle."

"They were at the end of the hall the whole time, Carolyn," said Cally. "When you opened my locker, they were all there, hiding around the corner, waiting for the fun." She paused a moment, then added, "Luce was with them."

Luce? Carolyn couldn't believe it. It couldn't be true. Luce would never stand by and let Pete or any of those creeps do anything like that to her.

"Where did you say you saw them?" she said to Mark. "Out in the parking lot?"

"I don't know if a confrontation is such a good idea right now," said Mark.

Carolyn opened the paper bag and carefully brought out the picture frame that belonged to Greatgran.

"It's ruined," she said as she handed it to Mark. "The pictures are completely ruined."

Mark stared silently at the blackened mess.

They were all there, leaning against one of the teachers' cars in the parking lot. Pete and some of the guys from the team and some of Pete's other friends and their girlfriends. And Luce. It looked to Carolyn as though they were reliving their little prank. Every few seconds a wave of laughter washed over the pack.

Luce didn't join in. Her face was solemn. But that made no difference to Carolyn. Besides Cally, Carolyn and possibly Orlando, Luce was the only other person who knew Cally's locker combination. Luce had seen Carolyn opening the locker, the way she'd seen Carolyn do maybe a hundred times before, and yet she hadn't called out to warn her. Having a grudge against Cally was one thing. Doing something like this was quite another.

Luce turned her head away when she saw Carolyn coming. Then she started to slip away.

"What's the matter, Luce?" Carolyn called. "Brave enough to pull a stunt like this, but too chicken to face up to it?"

Luce stopped walking, but she didn't turn around to face Carolyn.

"We were just helping the lovebirds along," Pete said innocently. He looked over at his buddies and laughed.

"Helping them?" Carolyn's eyes were rivetted to Luce's back.

"Sure," said Pete. "Hey, didn't you know? Orlando thinks he's white. He's dating a white girl. And poor old Cally, she thinks she's black. We were just making their wishes come true."

It made her sick. How did people get to be that stupid, she wondered, not to mention, that cruel.

She thought about arguing with him. She thought about asking him what possible difference it made to him or anyone else walking the face of the earth whether Orlando and Cally wanted to be friends. But her words would be wasted on him.

"Luce," she said to Luce's back.

Very slowly Luce turned. Her face was hard and cold. She stared impassively at Carolyn and said, "That's what you get when you hang around with those people."

Carolyn stared back. She wondered what it would feel like to punch Luce.

"Luce, you'll never know just how much damage you did today," she said. "And I don't think you even care."

"Listen, that Cally . . . "

Carolyn held up a hand. Luce jumped back, as if she thought Carolyn were going to hit her.

"I don't want to talk to you ever again," Carolyn said. "I just want you to know that as far as *I'm* concerned, it's over between us. And if you ever want to know why, don't bother asking. I don't believe I'll ever be prepared to tell you."

Carolyn turned and walked away.

Most of the time when Pete told the story, everyone laughed. It didn't matter how many times they had heard it before. It didn't even matter that they had been there when the paint splattered all over Carolyn. Pete and the guys thought the whole thing was hysterical. That was the really spooky part.

Luce knew she wouldn't be able to stop thinking about what was going to happen when they got to school the next day, how much trouble Pete was going to get into when this was reported, who else was going to get pulled into it. And whether she was going to be one of those people.

God, she wished Pete had never come up with the idea. He had been brooding over Carolyn, the way she had told him off. And then he had thought of the paint stacked up on the third floor. He'd mentioned it to some of the guys. And one of them, Arty Pryde, had said how his locker was next to Orlando's and he knew the combination. He'd made a point of watching. You never knew when the information would come in handy, the guy being the only nigger in school. And Pete had said, yeah, that would be good. Too bad nobody knows the chick's combo. And one by one the eyes had turned to Luce.

"Hey," one of them said, "you hang around with her,

and you girls always know each other's combinations."

And someone else had said, "Yeah. You know the combination, don't you, Luce?"

She didn't want to give them Cally's combination. She hadn't said no right then, though. I'll tell Pete later, is what she promised herself.

Next thing she knew, they had the paint, and a couple of guys were going to Orlando's locker. Then Pete turned to her. "So, what's the chick's combo?"

"I . . . I forget," she said.

Pete glowered at her.

"What do you mean, you forget? Come on, give us the combo!"

"No, honestly, I can't remember it."

Pete grabbed her by the arm and dragged her down the hallway. "What the fuck's the matter with you?"

"Pete, it's not my fault . . . "

"I know you know that combination. What I don't know is why you won't give it to me. Don't tell me you've got a thing for that nigger too."

"No, Pete. I just . . . "

"You just want to protect him, that's all." He pushed her against the lockers. "Fine. Have it your way. I'll find another way to do it. Without you."

"Pete . . . "

"I've had it with you, Luce. You don't know how to have fun, and you don't care about the things that are important to me. You care more about that god-damned jungle bunny."

"Pete . . . "

"I'm sick of you. We're through."

In the end, she gave him the combination.

Now she was going to be called down to the office and expelled. And her parents would probably kill her. For sure they would never let her see Pete again.

"Let's take the short cut," Carolyn said. She had rolled up the bottom of Mark's sweat pants, but they wouldn't stay rolled; they kept spilling down over her ankles.

"You mean, across the tracks and through the yard?" said Mark. He frowned. "It's not very safe."

"I don't care about safe," said Carolyn. "I care about fast. Besides, I've been crossing those tracks and cutting through the yard for practically my whole life. How dangerous could it be?"

She headed across the school parking lot in the direction of the path that cut through the woods beside the YMCA and led down the slope to the tracks. Mark strode along beside her.

"You really think we shouldn't report this?" Carolyn asked.

"Yeah, I do."

Carolyn glanced at his thin, handsome face. "I don't get it. You seem to think trouble is brewing, and yet you won't report it."

Mark shrugged. "Put yourself in Orlando's shoes," he said. "If some jerk was giving you a hard time, would you want to solve the problem yourself, or would it make you feel better to go running to the principal?"

"But you said yourself that his way could lead to more trouble," Carolyn said.

"I said if he tried to deal with it the way he dealt with what happened at the basketball game, it could lead to trouble."

Carolyn approached the railway tracks and paused to

peer first to her right, then to her left. "Nothing coming," she murmured.

Mark grasped her hand and hurried her across. His hand felt warm and strong.

As they began to climb a slope towards a rickety fence that enclosed an abandoned brick yard, Mark said, "I don't know what Orlando has in mind. From the way he looked, I'd say it wasn't gentle persuasion." He sighed as he helped Carolyn through a gap in the fence. "But then, Pete isn't a guy on whom gentle persuasion is likely to work." He squeezed through the opening after her.

The fence enclosed a large square area between the railway tracks and the highway. A network of small, overgrown pathways cut through the yard. One path led to a large tumbledown shack. Another led straight through an indentation in the ground to a second hole in the fence on the other side. A third climbed up to a ridge on which old crumbling bricks stood in piles. Some had been carried off by neighbourhood people. Others had been thrown about the yard by kids.

Carolyn usually took the most direct route, the one that led down into the indentation, but Mark laid a hand on her shoulder and said, "Let's go the other way. Up there."

Carolyn frowned. "This way's easier," she said, gesturing straight ahead.

"It's also wet," said Mark. Water from a recent rainstorm had turned the earth to thick mud.

"Don't walk too close to the edge," Mark cautioned as she climbed up the steep incline. "The ground isn't firm. They ought to move those bricks back before the ground gives way and they fall on someone."

111

It felt strange around school for the next couple of days. Creepy. Like lizards crawling up your back. Or waking up in the middle of the night and finding a spider taking a shortcut across your face. And the strangest part was Orlando.

The next day he said to Cally, "We're going to that dance on Saturday."

"What dance?"

"The one at school."

She frowned. "You said you didn't ever want to go to any dances at that school."

"I changed my mind."

She stared at him. He was talking to her with a kind of flat voice, like he was a robot.

"Why did you change your mind?" she asked. He had turned on her.

"What's the matter?" he demanded. "Scared to go to the dance with me? Scared all your little white friends will give you a hard time if they see you dancing with a nigger?"

"Orlando!"

He was staring at her like he hated her.

"I'll go with you," she said. "I'm not afraid."

Except that she was afraid. Not of being seen with him, but of what was going to happen at the dance.

"You're going to the dance?" Tell me it's not true, Carolyn had thought. Or, if it has to be true, let it be the Christmas dance she's talking about. Maybe things will have cooled down a little by Christmas.

"He wants to go," Cally had replied. "And I can't think of one good reason why he shouldn't."

"Except that Pete is going," said Carolyn. "And he'll probably want to kill Orlando."

Cally had looked a little scared then. But she obviously hadn't let her fear get the better of her because there she was now, coming through the gym doors on Orlando's arm. Orlando stood tall and kept his eyes straight ahead, like he wasn't interested in seeing anyone. Beside him in a pale-blue dress, Cally looked small and fragile. Her eyes darted around the room; there was no smile on her trembling lips as she walked with Orlando towards Mark and Carolyn.

Mark took a sip of his punch and nodded at Orlando.

"Nice party," Orlando said. Nothing in his voice indicated that he meant it.

It got to Carolyn, the way he said it, and the way his eyes started moving slowly around the gym, counterclockwise, looking at face after face, like a sharp old gunfighter, looking for a foolish young rival. She moved a little closer to Mark.

Orlando put an arm around Cally and said, "Let's dance." There was no joy in Cally's face as Orlando steered her out onto the dance floor. Her eyes had focussed in on one end of the gym, a patch under the basketball net where Pete was swaying to the music with Luce in his arms. As Carolyn watched, she could see that Orlando was guiding Cally slowly, inexorably, in that same direction.

"Come on," she said, taking Mark's hand. "Let's dance."

Mark followed behind, and when she eased him across the floor in Cally and Orlando's wake, he said, "Who's leading here anyway?"

Carolyn nodded to where Pete and Orlando were. The gap between the two was closing.

"I didn't want to be any part of this," Mark said. But he stayed with her as she inched closer to the two enemies.

Anyone who didn't know Orlando and what had happened between him and Pete would have seen nothing because all Orlando did was dance close enough to Pete for long enough, and Pete did what Carolyn would have predicted he would. He got mad and shoved Orlando. Orlando pushed Cally behind him to protect her, and he looked at Pete. "It's such a nice party. Shame to ruin it."

"Yeah," said Pete. "Suppose we have our own party. Outside."

Orlando nodded.

Luce didn't even try to stop Pete. She just stared at him, then she stared at Carolyn. Or it was more like she stared through Carolyn.

But Cally held onto Orlando. "Don't go," she pleaded. "Stay here, Orlando. Or we can go home, if you want to."

He was gentle as he peeled her hands off his arm. Then he set her at arm's length and held her there a moment as if she were a china figurine. Then he started to walk across the gym floor behind Pete. Carolyn, Mark and Cally followed, Carolyn holding onto Cally's arm to restrain her.

"I'm going to get someone," said Mark. But when he tried to turn away, he found his path blocked by a couple of Pete's friends.

"Don't," one of them said.

They went out the rear doors and onto the playing field behind the gym, where it was dark. The only illumination came from one floodlight, focussed on a small area of ground. Orlando walked to the very edge of the light. Pete stayed close to the wall, watching him. Then Orlando turned to face Pete.

Pete smiled. He took a couple of steps forward, moving in a crouch, like a wild animal. He had a glint in his eyes, and Carolyn could barely stand to watch. Then, suddenly, Orlando snapped his fingers. The sound cracked through the air like a rifle shot. Carolyn jumped as a dozen black guys stepped forward out of the darkness and into the edge of the floodlit ground. Pete stopped dead in his tracks.

"What's the matter?" said Orlando. "You don't like the odds?"

A cruel smile eradicated the surprise that had registered on Pete's face. Pete snapped his fingers. More than a dozen of Pete's friends stepped forward.

"Now I'm definitely going for help," said Mark. He broke away from Carolyn and made for the door.

Orlando began to move towards Pete and the two circled each other, arms out in front of them, knees bent, eyes locked on each other. Pete made the first move, just as Carolyn had known he would. He ploughed out with his fist, but Orlando slipped to the right; the fist missed its mark, Orlando got a grip on the arm and twisted it up and back. Then all hell broke loose. Orlando's friends were pummelling Pete's friends, and they were being pummelled in return.

"We've got to stop them," Cally screamed.

She started to move forward. Carolyn grabbed her. "You're nuts. You're going to get hurt!"

The gym door clanged open and more people plunged into the fight, men in suits this time. Teachers. Pulling guys off guys.

"Oh no," moaned Cally. She broke free of Carolyn's grip and ran forward. Orlando was lying motionless on the ground, face up. There was a pool of blood beside his head.

9

"*H*ow's Orlando doing?" asked Carolyn. She always made a point of asking. Not many others did. Cally appreciated Carolyn's concern.

"He's getting better," she said.

Physically speaking, that was true. At first, when she had gone to the hospital and had seen him with that huge bandage around his head, and he was in such pain, she had thought that was the worst. They told him it had been a bad concussion and fracture and that he'd have to stay in the hospital a while. Then he picked up an infection that ran his temperature up to a hundred and four and they made him stay in for ten days on top of the three weeks he had already been there. But what Cally hadn't bargained for was what would happen when he came home.

He hadn't been a picnic in the hospital. Especially when he heard he had been suspended from school along with Pete, and that the incident was being put on his record as well as on Pete's. He was ready to strangle Mr. Jamieson, the principal.

"If all those guys hadn't been there with you," Cally said, "it would have been different. He would have only suspended Pete."

"Are you saying I should have let Pete pound me out?" said Orlando. "You telling me that would have been better?"

Cally's face burned. "Of course not. But Mr. Jamieson doesn't like the idea of gangs . . . "

"Who said anything about gangs?" Orlando was sitting up straight in bed, his eyes blacker than the paint that had covered Carolyn.

"That's the way Mr. Jamieson saw it," Cally said patiently. "He saw Pete with a bunch of guys and you with a bunch of guys, and he thought about what happened on the basketball court that time . . . "

"Oh, great," said Orlando, flourishing a hand under her nose. "I hang around with my friends and all of a sudden I'm a gang leader."

Cally bit her lip as she studied his fury. "Your friends were hanging around out behind the school," she said at last, her voice low, her eyes focussed on the crisp white of his sheet. She didn't dare look at him. "They were waiting for something to happen."

He was silent for so long that she had to look at him. Then she was sorry she had. His eyes were burning, his lips set in disdain.

"You knew something was going to happen, didn't you?" she asked.

He was staring at her with those dark eyes of his, silent as a rock. She felt like shaking him.

"The school board almost voted to expel you," she said. "Both of you. There were a lot of people who said they wanted to make it clear that they wouldn't put up with fighting like that."

She had heard it all, word for word, from Mrs. Burns, her mother's friend. Mr. Burns was a school trustee. And

118

Mrs. Burns hadn't wasted much time getting over to talk to Cally's mother about it. Nor had Mr. Curran dragged his heels. He and Casper had been down at the end of the driveway first thing the morning after the fight, and while Casper tugged at his chain, Mr. Curran had gravely discussed with Cally's mother "that terrible situation up at the school."

"You're lucky Mr. Jamieson stuck up for you, and that it's only a suspension."

"I wasn't going to let him push me around anymore," said Orlando. "I have as much right to be here as he does."

"Nobody's saying you don't."

He arched his brows. "Nobody?"

Well, she thought, maybe Mr. Curran. And Mrs. Burns. And . . . "It could have been worse, Orlando. You really could have been expelled."

Now that Orlando was at home, his mood hadn't improved. In two days the Christmas holidays would begin. Orlando hadn't planned on going back to school until January. Now, the way he was talking, it looked as though he might never go back.

"Why should I?" he asked Cally. "What's the percentage?"

"But you don't want to look like you're running away."

Orlando snorted. "You sound like my father. He says I have to go back to prove they can't scare me."

"I think your father's right."

"I don't care what they think," Orlando said. "I don't like them. They don't like me. And I don't want to spend the rest of my life having to put up with their shit."

"What'll you do? Go downtown to the same school as your cousin Carlene?"

He nodded. "I guess."

"And then? Where do you go after that?"

He scowled at her. "What do you mean?"

"What do you want to do after high school? Go to university maybe? Get a degree? Maybe a PhD like your father? Or maybe go to medical school or law school. How many black medical students do you think there are at McGill? Or black law students? You think there aren't more people like Pete out there who are going to give you a hard time?"

He stared at her. "You must have got some black paint on you," he said. "You sound just like my father."

"You have to go back, Orlando."

"I don't have to do anything I don't want to," he said.

Carolyn was up in her room, Christmas wrapping paper, scissors and ribbon strewn across her bed, when she heard a scream.

Mrs. Quaid was down in the kitchen making short-bread cookies. At first Carolyn thought she was the one who had been screaming. But when she pelted down the stairs, there was her mother in her apron, a smudge of flour on her nose. She was heading for the back room. Carolyn raced after her.

The door to Greatgran's room was open. It looked like a tornado had swirled through the room. Greatgran was in a corner next to a small bureau. She was ransacking its drawers, yanking them open and throwing everything out. Behind her, shrieking at her to stop, was Grandma Dell.

Carolyn's mother screeched to a halt just inside the

door and surveyed the scene. "What on earth . . . " Carolyn heard her whisper in a near-reverential tone. Carolyn almost collided into the back of her, she stopped so quickly. Then Mrs. Quaid lurched forward, wading in among the litter and over to the two women.

"What's the matter?" she asked.

"She's looking for something," said Grandma Dell.

A hairbrush came sailing out of a drawer and narrowly missed Mrs. Quaid's head.

"What is she looking for?" asked Carolyn.

"Whatever it is," said Carolyn's mother, "I suggest we help her find it before she ruins her room completely."

"A picture," said Grandma Dell. "She's looking for a picture."

A picture. Carolyn's heart slowed. The picture Greatgran had given to Mark. The picture that had been soaked in oily black paint.

Greatgran slammed one emptied drawer and wrenched open another.

Grandma Dell reached out and tried to pin Greatgran's arms to her sides, but Greatgran broke free and ripped another drawer open so forcefully that it came out of the bureau, toppling her backward into Grandma Dell. If Carolyn's mother hadn't stepped in, both would have crashed to the floor.

"She's going to hurt herself if she keeps this up," said Grandma Dell.

"In that case," said Mrs. Quaid as Greatgran rooted through the drawer on the floor, "let's find that picture."

"We can't," Grandma Dell said quietly.

Carolyn held her breath.

"Why not?" said Mrs. Quaid.

121

"Because the picture she's looking for doesn't exist anymore. It hasn't existed for, Lord, most of my lifetime, I'm sure. It's gone. Destroyed."

Mrs. Quaid's eyebrows arched. She didn't have the vaguest idea what her mother was talking about.

Greatgran ripped a row of books from the shelf beside her bed. They crashed to the floor.

"Mother, for heaven's sake," cried Grandma Dell.

"Mother," said Mrs. Quaid, gently grasping Grandma Dell by the shoulders, "why don't you go into the kitchen with Carolyn? I'm sure she would make you a cup of tea."

"But, Elizabeth, she's tearing the place apart."

"Please, Mother," said Mrs. Quaid. "I think I can handle this."

Grandma Dell swayed a little on her feet. Carolyn stepped towards her, afraid she was going to fall.

"Carolyn," said Mrs. Quaid, "take Grandma Dell into the kitchen and make her a cup of tea. I'll be along in a few minutes."

Grandma Dell's face was pale. She picked her way gingerly across the debris-filled room and into the front hall. Carolyn followed her into the kitchen and put the kettle on.

Grandma Dell sank into a chair and pulled a vial from her pocket. Carolyn watched out of the corner of her eye as Grandma Dell popped a pill into her mouth, leaned back and closed her eyes.

When Carolyn finally brought her a cup of tea, she opened her eyes and looked a little refreshed.

"Thank you, dear," she said as she stirred sugar into the cup. She took a sip and smiled appreciatively at Carolyn.

Carolyn thought: it's now or never.

"Could I ask you a question, Grandma Dell?" she said. "You don't have to answer if you don't want to. But there's something I want to know."

Grandma Dell looked quizzically at her. "I suppose I could try," she said at last.

Carolyn took a deep breath, as she always did when she was unsure of herself. "What happened to Great-gran's sister Kathleen?"

Grandma Dell's head snapped back. Her eyes popped open so wide Carolyn thought her eyeballs might drop out. The cup shook in her hands. "What do you know about that?"

She was surprised by the ferocity of her grandmother's reaction. "Just that she had a sister and her name was Kathleen," said Carolyn.

Grandma Dell regarded her icily over the rim of her teacup.

"That's the picture she's looking for, isn't it?" asked Carolyn. "A picture of Kathleen."

"You know quite a lot," said Grandma Dell as she set her cup back into its saucer. "You know more than your own mother knows."

Grandma Dell sank back into her chair. She pressed her thumb and forefinger to the bridge of her nose and closed her eyes. Then, as her hand dropped back into her lap, she sighed.

"Do you know much about Ireland?" she asked.

"A little. I know there's fighting going on over there."

Grandma Dell nodded. "In the north, yes. There's fighting. Have you ever heard of the Easter Uprising?"

Carolyn shook her head.

"Well, that happened a long time ago. In 1916, to be exact. During the First World War. You see, what they're fighting for in the north now is independence. They want to be completely free from England."

Carolyn nodded. She did current events in school, so she knew a little about that.

"Well, when Greatgran was a girl, all of Ireland was ruled by the British. And there were plenty of Irish who didn't think that was right. In 1916 some of the more militant ones staged an uprising to try to drive the British out of Ireland. It failed, of course. They were hopelessly outnumbered. But that didn't stop folks from wanting their independence."

"There," said Mrs. Quaid's voice from the doorway to the kitchen. She held Greatgran by the elbow and steered her towards the table. "Why don't you sit down here, Gran, and I'll finish up. Carolyn will pour you a cup of tea." She glanced at Carolyn. "Won't you, dear?"

Carolyn jumped up to fetch another cup and saucer while her mother settled Greatgran into a chair. As Carolyn poured the tea, her mother disappeared into Greatgran's room.

Carolyn took her place at the table and glanced at Grandma Dell, who was peering over the rim of her teacup at Greatgran.

Greatgran's thin grey hair stuck out at odd angles. She raised a hand to try to smooth it back into place. Then she took a sip of tea.

"I heard you talking about the Rising," Greatgran said. "You know your father doesn't like to hear talk about that."

Grandma Dell sighed and shook her head. "For pity sake, Mother, Father's been dead for years."

Greatgran peered at her. "Don't you think I know

that?" she said with a snort. "And mind your tone when you talk to your mother." She paused a moment, then added, "You *were* talking about the Rising."

Grandma Dell started to shake her head again. Then she sighed and shrugged. "All right," she said, "yes. I was talking about the Rising. Carolyn asked me about it." She nodded towards Carolyn.

"Oh," said Greatgran, "Carolyn." She stretched her hand across the table and squeezed Carolyn's hand. Both the unexpectedness of the gesture and the chill of Greatgran's skin startled Carolyn. "Don't you know about the Rising, Carolyn? Don't they teach you young people anything in school these days?"

The lilt in her voice was unfamiliar; her smile was fragile, polite. Carolyn realized that Greatgran didn't know who she was.

"My family's from Ireland," Greatgran continued. "I was there at the time of the Rising."

Grandma Dell sighed again; she shrugged helplessly at Carolyn.

"I was just telling her that, Mother," she said.

"Well," said Greatgran, "don't let me interrupt you." She leaned back in her chair, her slim white hands clasped on the table.

Grandma Dell looked at Carolyn. "All the Uprising accomplished," she continued, "was to make the British more nervous. They started rounding up everyone they suspected of being an Irish nationalist. They put one of my father's cousins into prison. A man from our village was hanged. Well, that stirred things up even more. Folks who had been peaceful at first became angry when innocent sons and husbands were rounded up by the British."

She sighed. "Then there were those who were never so peaceful. Like my grandfather and father. Fierce Irishmen, proud of their country."

"He could be a hateful man," Greatgran said grimly.

Grandma Dell stared at her. "Who?" she said.

"Your father. He could be a hateful man. He was hateful towards William. And Kathleen."

Grandma Dell stiffened in her chair. "He was a man who stood up for what he believed," she said. "He was a man of fire."

"Fire," Greatgran said bitterly. Her mouth twisted sourly. "Fire, yes. He threw all that was left of Kathleen into the fire."

"He did it for you," said Grandma Dell. "He did it to help you."

"Help me?" Greatgran spat the word out. She turned to Carolyn. "My sister Kathleen fell in love with a boy whose father was British. William was born in Ireland. Raised there, on the same soil as the rest of us. But because his father was British, my father forbade Kathleen to have anything to do with him." She gazed at Carolyn as if through a mist. "You know, dear," she said, "you remind me a great deal of Kathleen. I can see it in your eyes, in your mouth."

"Mother, please . . . " said Grandma Dell.

"Mother, please," parroted Greatgran. She sighed. "My own father was thought to be a man of some fire himself. He wouldn't let Kathleen out of the house unless I went with her, unless I reported back to him everything she did, every word she spoke." When she looked over at Carolyn again, her eyes were distant. "I lied to him, didn't I, Kathleen? I would tell him we went into the village

126

when really you would slip off into the woods with William." She smiled. "You were so flushed when you'd come back, and you'd hum the rest of the day through your chores. Oh, I used to be so jealous of you, Kathleen O'Donnell. The most beautiful girl in the village, all the boys ate out of your hand. And now you had found this sweet gentle young man. I used to wish I had a young man like your William. Not one who'd come home every night smelling of whiskey."

Watching her eyes was like watching a summer storm come up. They were clear and blue at first, and her smile was the sun that illuminated them. Then they clouded, and the clouds turned from grey to black.

"Father was wrong to oppose the wedding. He was wrong to turn you out of the house. If it hadn't been for Father, none of it would have happened."

She fell silent.

Carolyn glanced at Grandma Dell. "What happened?" she asked eagerly.

Grandma Dell shrugged. "I only know what I've been told by my uncles and aunts," she said. "They say the O'Donnell boys rounded up some men and they went off to stop the wedding." She glanced over at Greatgran. "They all tell me that your great-grandmother was every bit as beautiful as Kathleen in those days, that they were the most beautiful women in the county and all the men adored them. At the wedding, when the angry young men turned up, Kathleen stepped forward and told the band to start playing. Then she whispered something into your great-grandmother's ear."

"That you did," said Greatgran, smiling fondly again. "I admit, I thought you were mad. Dance, you said. Men with their fists clenched all around us, and you have the musicians strike up a waltz and you tell me, dance with William."

"Mother danced with Kathleen's new husband," said Grandma Dell. "And Kathleen danced with my father. They say it was a sight to see. Two rows of angry men, fists ready to start swinging, ranged against each other. And in the middle the two beautiful O'Donnell sisters. Kathleen took my father's hand and drew him close to her and wouldn't let him go. What could the poor man do? He was too much of a gentleman to throw a bride to the ground. They say he danced reluctantly at first. Then, I don't know whether it was the music or the look in Kathleen's eyes, but whatever it was, when the dance was over Kathleen kissed him on the cheek and he left, taking his men with him. There was no trouble that night."

"That sounds like a happy ending," Carolyn said. She could just see it, the two brave and beautiful O'Donnell sisters keeping the peace with a song and a dance.

"A few months later a bomb went off in the house where Kathleen and William lived. They were both killed. Mother cried and carried on for so long that her family feared for the life of the child she was carrying. Me. Just after I was born, my father sent her to a sanitorium to get well. While she was away, my father burned every picture of Kathleen he could get his hands on. He wanted Mother to be able to forget Kathleen."

Across the table Greatgran sniffled. Tears trickled down her cheeks.

"Kathleen," she sobbed. "My picture."

Grandma Dell looked at her ancient mother. "I'm sorry," she whispered. "But I remember how you used to cry. I remember it so well from when I was little. You'd be standing in the kitchen peeling potatoes, and all of a sudden you would start to cry. Father would tell me it was Kathleen who'd come to you again."

She took Greatgran's hand, and the two of them stared into each other's eyes. Carolyn had never really thought of them as mother and daughter. It had never occurred to her what they had been through together over the past sixty years.

"I'm sorry, Mother," said Grandma Dell. And for the first time Carolyn saw her shed a tear.

"Greatgran," Carolyn said softly, "I know what happened to your picture."

10

Christmas Day had been the absolute worst. Orlando had waited until Christmas Eve to drop the bomb on her: no way he was going back to that school. They argued. It was the same argument they'd been having over and over again, ever since he had first mentioned the possibility of a transfer.

"You don't understand," he told her bitterly. "You don't understand and you'll never understand."

She had been trying to understand. She thought she could at least imagine what it must be like to be so alone among so many people, to be so different.

"But it's not everyone," she told him. "There are a lot of people who don't agree with what Pete did."

His stare had chilled her. "A *lot* of people? Name ten."

"Me," she said. "And Carolyn. And Mark . . ." Her voice trailed off.

Orlando kept staring at her, waiting. "I'll make it easier," he said after a while. "Name five."

"I don't know a lot of people. I'm not one of those people who have tons of friends."

"It's my life and I'm not going back there."

"Where will you go?"

"Downtown."

"I'll never see you."

His face softened a little, but he didn't actually smile. "I live right next door, Cally."

"If you go downtown, you'll have to leave early in the morning. And you'll get home real late, especially if you're on the basketball team there . . . "

He slipped an arm around her, and they sat quietly for a minute or two.

Cally went home and tried to look cheerful, even if she didn't feel it inside. It was Christmas. A time of good cheer. Peace on earth and all that stuff. But when she climbed into bed that night, the tears began to flow, and all the things she hadn't said flooded her mind.

Like, if he was going downtown to school, he'd be back with all his friends. All day. Every day. He'd be with other girls. Girls who *did* understand. Girls who knew exactly what he was talking about. And she'd be alone. It wasn't fair. It just wasn't fair. And it was all Pete's fault. Pete and Luce.

She called Carolyn the next day, thinking she would explode if she couldn't get it out. But all she did was wish Carolyn a merry Christmas. Carolyn sounded thrilled that Mark's family had stopped over for a Christmas drink, and there was laughter in the background. She doesn't want to hear about my problems, Cally thought.

The holidays passed.

On the first day of school Cally trudged through the snow to Carolyn's house.

"So he's really transferring, huh?"

Cally nodded. Her lower lip began to tremble.

Carolyn pulled a wad of tissues out of her pocket and pressed it into Cally's mittened hand.

"Maybe it's for the best," Carolyn said.

Cally's eyes blazed. "Whose best?" she snapped.

Carolyn looked startled. "I'm sorry. But I guess it hasn't been easy for him."

Cally wiped her eyes angrily and blew her nose. They walked to school in awkward silence.

It was strange pulling open the big front doors and stepping inside after being away for two weeks. It was strange seeing all those people stashing their boots and coats in their lockers, digging out books for the first few classes of the day, everyone looking relaxed because exams were behind them now, they didn't even have to worry about homework assignments, not today. People talking about their holidays and Christmas presents and the New Year's parties they had gone to. Life going on. And nobody thinking, hmmm, I wonder what happened to that black kid.

Pete was hanging out in the front hall.

"Maybe he hasn't heard," Carolyn muttered.

Cally glanced at him and at Luce, who was standing beside him, her arm around his waist. They were both frowning at her. Cally thought for a moment that Luce was going to talk to her. And, instead of dreading it, she wished Luce would. She wished Luce would say something like, where's your boyfriend? Because then Cally could say something back to her, tell her right in front of everybody exactly what she thought of her. Embarrass her maybe, if not hurt her.

But Luce's mouth snapped shut again. And Cally's body went slack. Probably she wouldn't have been able to think of a bitchy thing to say. Luce would have had the perfect comeback, and Pete and all his friends would have laughed at Cally.

Then Luce was nudging Pete. And Pete's head was turning towards the front door, and the more he turned, the more his chin sagged. He started to step forward, but Luce had a hand wrapped around him; she held him back.

Beside Cally, Carolyn murmured, "Jesus."

Cally turned to see Orlando come through the door, books under his arm, head held high, serious, grim-faced. He strode up to her, took her by the hand and led her down the hall past Pete, past Luce, past everyone, down to her locker.

Luce had been relieved when she heard the rumour going around. They were saying that Orlando wasn't coming back to school; that he had transferred downtown. Luce had thought, thank God. Pete had slammed his fist into the wall; she was surprised he didn't smash it.

"He's gone," she had said. "He won't be on the team anymore."

"Yeah," said Pete. He was rubbing his sore hand, breathing heavily. "Yeah, he's gone."

He talked about it for days afterward. "Coward," he'd say to her, to his friends, to anyone who would listen and even to people who didn't seem to care. "The guy's a coward. He couldn't stand the heat. He ran away."

After a while he calmed down.

When they walked to school that first day after the New Year, Pete had been unusually quiet. And when they got there, he had insisted they wait around at the front door. She didn't ask why; she didn't want an argument. And, anyway, she knew. She could feel the muscles in his abdomen relax when Cally came through the front door with Carolyn, without Orlando.

When she saw those two again, especially Carolyn, she wanted to go up to them and say something. Orlando was gone. Hey, guys, can't we just let bygones be bygones? She'd almost stepped forward, but something in their eyes stopped her. Carolyn glanced at her the way a person might glance at a slug in the garden. Cally was different. She had poison in her eyes; she was a venomous snake who would strike given the chance. Luce wished Orlando had never existed.

And then, it couldn't be – there he was. Her hand closed involuntarily on Pete's waist. Pete glanced at her, then followed her gaze to the door. She thought he was going to topple over when he saw Orlando; he went so rigid, he seemed to stop breathing. Then, after Orlando had taken Cally by the hand and led her away, Pete turned to her and very slowly a smile broke out across his face.

"Pete, you're not going to do anything, are you?"

"Me?" said Pete. He didn't even try to put a gloss of innocence on the word.

She wasn't sure what to expect that day. She walked through the hallways holding her breath, waiting for the roof to cave in. When she was actually in class, she wondered what Pete was up to, if *it* had happened yet.

But nothing happened.

She was so relieved when, at the end of the school day, she came down the hallway and saw him leaning there against her locker with a bunch of guys from the team, waiting for her.

"You want to go somewhere?" she asked. "Down to the village?"

"Too cold," he said. "I thought we'd all go over to my place, maybe order a pizza. Interested?"

She smiled. If he was thinking of going down to his rec room, of fooling around over a pizza, then he wasn't thinking about Orlando. He wasn't thinking about trouble.

It was almost dark outside when they left school. She hated that about January and February. The days were so short that she spent her only sunlight hours indoors, in class. The sun had barely cleared the tree tops when she walked to school in the morning; the street lights were on by the time she left it in the afternoon. She was looking forward to spring.

Then the wind came up and the snow started to fall. It danced and swirled and blinded her when she raised her head. They walked in silence, heads bowed, probably all thinking about the same thing she was: the warmth of Pete's rec room, the heat of a fresh pizza.

They circled around to the side of the school, cut along the pathway that ran alongside the Y and down the hill to the railway tracks.

"Jesus Murphy, it's cold," muttered Pete.

The wind was howling and it blasted the snow even harder. Not soft downy flakes of snow, but icy pellets driven by the wind, stinging their faces like bullets.

"Come on," said Pete, his hand closing around Luce's. "Let's move it a little."

He guided her to the hole in the fence around the brick yard. She could see the wind blowing into footprints on the other side and guessed other kids had had the same idea: cut through the brick yard and across the tracks to get home fast, even though probably every kid in St. Jacques had been warned by his mother not to take that route. The brick yard was abandoned and in ill repair, the railway tracks were hazardous, and a kid had been killed there a couple of years back, run over by a train. But that never stopped some kids, kids who needed a short cut and who thought, that can never happen to me.

They climbed single file up the rim of the yard and made their way along the top ridge where stacks of decaying bricks still sat, covered in snow. The cold wind had put a crust on the ice, through which Luce's feet fell with every step. She staggered and stumbled and had to grope for a handhold. She clawed at a stack of bricks, her whole weight falling against them. The stack gave a little. Luce gasped. She could see the bricks falling into the void.

"You okay?" said Pete, grabbing her by the elbow and pulling her back to her feet.

"Yeah," she said. Her breathing was laboured. "It's so slippery up here, Pete." She gazed down, way down, thinking, I could have gone over there. I could have hit the ground below, head first.

A shadow caught her eye. She stared through the gathering storm.

"There's someone down there," she said. A chill stole through her. "I could have killed someone."

Pete picked his way over to the edge of the ridge and peered down. He stood motionless, staring, and then he smiled.

"Well," he said to her and all the guys, "what do you know about that? If it isn't our friendly neighbourhood jungle bunny."

Luce's eyes widened. She stared. It was Orlando. Making his way cautiously through the yard. Taking the same short cut they were.

Pete was edging along the rim, following Orlando from above, keeping right on top of him. Luce scrambled over to him. The guys moved up a little, but not too close to Pete.

"What are you going to do? Pete, you're not going to do anything, are you?"

Pete was moving towards a stack of bricks. She could see Orlando down below, making his way laboriously over the ice-glazed snow, the wind swirling around him.

"Pete . . . "

"The guy needs a little scare. He's too cocky." He looked past her to the guys, searching their faces. He wants them to agree, she thought.

"But, Pete . . . "

"For Christ's sake, I'm not going to hurt him. I'm just going to show him a guy can't be too careful."

And his whole weight was pushing against the bricks, heaving them to the edge where the earth and the snow started to crumble.

She screamed. She screamed Orlando's name and saw him look up and she thought: my God, what have I done? Because he just stood down there, not moving, staring up through the ice and the snow and the gloom. If he didn't move . . .

She leapt at Pete, thinking to get him away from the bricks, to push him back. He side-stepped her neatly. As she fell, she saw him give the final push to the bricks. She screamed again when Pete pushed her, she screamed as the bricks slipped off the edge, and she was still screaming when Pete started to laugh.

The guys from the team said nothing, did nothing. It was as though they had been frozen into mute statues by

138

the cold and the wind. The only thing Luce could see was the glaze of shock on each pair of eyes.

Carolyn was sitting at the dining-room table. Mark sat opposite her. Greatgran sat next to her, turning over puzzle pieces. Mark was picking through the twelve hundred pieces, looking for all the bits of edge, shoving them across to her. Carolyn was trying to fit them together, but it wasn't easy. Everything looked the same.

"You could have got a scene of Niagara Falls," she said. "Or at least something with people in it, so we could get some kind of idea what goes where."

Mark laughed. "Don't blame me," he said. "I didn't pick it. Santa Claus did. I guess he knows I like pizza."

That's what the puzzle was. A giant pepperoni and mushroom pizza.

Carolyn sighed. She started to get up when the doorbell rang, but her mother breezed out of the kitchen, wiping her hands on her apron, and called out in a singsong voice, "I'll get it." She was back a moment later, looking at Carolyn. "You've got company."

"Cally?" said Carolyn, looking up. The smile vanished from her face when she saw Luce standing there in the hallway, smiling shakily at her.

"Hi," she said in a voice so low Carolyn could hardly hear her.

Carolyn regarded her icily, then glanced at her mother. Mrs. Quaid frowned. She didn't know what was going on.

"Can we talk for a moment?" Luce said. She glanced around nervously. "In private?"

Carolyn wanted to say no, tell her to go to hell. Luce

was the last person she wanted to have anything to do with. But her mother was standing right there. And Greatgran was smiling over at Luce. Carolyn glanced at Mark. Mark nodded.

"I'll be back in a minute," Carolyn said as she stood up. Luce followed her quietly up the stairs.

When she got to her room, Carolyn flopped down onto her bed. Luce just stood there awkwardly in the middle of the room, biting her lip and glancing around. Carolyn said nothing; no way she was going to make this easy for her.

"I dumped Pete," Luce said at last.

Carolyn frowned as she studied the girl. "You expect me to believe that?" she said at last. "*You* dumped him?"

Luce's face turned purple. She stared down at her feet a moment, then said, "Okay, so the literal truth is, he dumped me."

"Break my heart," Carolyn said acidly. She stared venomously at Luce. Who did she think she was that she could just waltz in and expect to be welcomed with open arms?

"Carolyn . . . " A tiny voice. A tremulous voice. Carolyn stared at her; inside she was shaking with rage. "Aw, Carolyn, come on. Say something. Please?"

Say something? Jeeze, didn't she know when she was well off? If Carolyn said anything, anything at all, it would be something angry. Something maybe even hurtful. She wished Luce hadn't come over in the first place. Then she wouldn't be stuck in her room with her, just wishing she would go away but not knowing exactly how to get rid of her.

"Carolyn . . . "

"What do you want me to say, Luce? You want me to say, forget it? Let's be friends again? Is that what you want to hear? Because if it is . . . "

Luce turned and ran. Carolyn listened to her feet thumping down two flights of stairs and wondered what her mother would think.

11

She awoke with a start. It was as if she had been falling, falling, falling endlessly. Then she hit bottom. She thought she screamed, but when she sat up, sweat pouring from her face, peering into the blackness of her room, she didn't hear a sound. Surely if she had screamed, she would have awakened her mother. She would have awakened somebody.

She'd been having nightmares regularly, ever since Pete had pushed the bricks down and narrowly missed Orlando.

Sometimes she found herself wondering if that had really happened. It was so easy to believe it hadn't, all the darkness and cold that had surrounded it, and the driving snow, it was like being in a fog.

She thought Pete had killed him. Pete had shoved her to the ground and she had crawled to the edge of the ridge and had peered down. Orlando had peered back up, but his eyes were fixed on Pete, not her. Maybe he hadn't even seen her. He had just stood down there, looking up, until Pete took a couple of steps back from the edge, removing himself from Orlando's line of vision.

She had stumbled to her feet and stood there, shivering, her teeth chattering from the cold, while under her jacket she could feel sweat running down her back.

"You could have killed him," she said, her voice hoarse, strangled. "You could have fucking killed him."

Pete stared back at her, his face white, his eyes glazed. She began to wonder if he was even breathing. She turned and stumbled away.

She couldn't sleep all that night. She just kept thinking about the bricks, and she found herself gazing forever into Orlando's upturned face, into his cold black eyes.

She thought she should do something about it, but didn't know what. Tell her parents? Tell the cops? What if Pete did it again?

"Pete?" He was at his locker and didn't turn when she called his name.

She circled around to where she could see him. "Pete?"

He didn't answer.

"Pete, I don't think we should see each other anymore."

He looked up with blank eyes, vacant eyes. And she knew he wasn't going to disagree. He sure wasn't going to beg for forgiveness or gush out an apology.

"As far as I'm concerned," he said, "you're history."

And that was that.

Tears blinded her eyes as she walked away. She hated herself for crying. But then it wasn't really Pete she was crying for. It was everything.

Cally looked across the cafeteria at Pete and shuddered. She looked back at Orlando. "He really gives me the creeps," she said.

"That's because he *is* a creep," said Carolyn.

Mark, who was sitting across the table from her, next to Orlando, nodded.

Cally stole another peek at Pete. He was sitting two tables over in the cafeteria and hadn't taken his eyes off the back of Orlando's head. "He just keeps staring. What's he up to?"

"Don't sweat it," Orlando said. He stretched a hand across the table and took one of hers in his. Cally blushed. She always blushed when Orlando touched her in public. "He's just trying to psyche me out, that's all."

"That's what's so creepy," said Cally, shivering. "I almost wish he'd *do* something."

Mark shook his head. "When Pete *does* something," he said, "it's usually bad news."

"His record isn't that great right now," said Orlando. "Four at bats. One win, two ties, one loss."

"That's not the way I count it," said Carolyn.

"Me either," said Cally.

Orlando shrugged. "He sent me to the hospital. A definite win. The basketball game I consider a draw – he lost as much as he won. Same with the paint thing. The guy could only gloat so much as long as I wasn't making a big deal about it."

"And the loss?" said Cally.

"The bricks."

"Bricks? What bricks?"

A strange look crossed Orlando's face. He looked down at the table top.

"What bricks?" Cally repeated.

It took him a full minute before he looked up at her again. Then, his face grim, he told her what had happened in the brick yard.

Cally's face turned white. "You could have been killed."

145

"The way I see it," said Orlando, "I would have been. If it hadn't been for that scream."

"Scream?"

"Someone screamed. Pete's girlfriend, I think."

Carolyn leaned forward across the table. "Luce was there?"

Orlando nodded.

"Carolyn?" She had never thought one word could be so hard to speak. She looked at Carolyn's back and said again, "Carolyn, can I talk to you? Please?"

Carolyn turned slowly from her locker. Her face was as cold and dark as an Arctic night. "Go away," she said.

"Come on, Carolyn. Please? Just listen to me for five minutes?"

Carolyn slipped into her coat, slung her purse over her shoulder and slammed her locker door shut.

"I've known you since the second grade," said Luce. "Come on, don't I at least rate a second chance?"

"He could have killed Orlando."

Luce stared slack-jawed at her friend. The first time she had tried to talk to Carolyn, she realized that Orlando had said nothing about the incident in the brick yard. It was clear now that he had finally told the story.

"I know," she said quietly. Tears gathered in her eyes, even though she had vowed to remain calm. "Carolyn, I'm sorry."

"Sorry doesn't cut it, Luce."

"I'm not seeing him anymore."

Carolyn stared, her gaze like ice.

"It was a mistake, okay? I didn't know he would do something like that. I didn't know."

146

As Carolyn turned away from her, Luce began to sob. She tried to will herself to stop, but the floodgates had already opened, and the force of the water was too great to restrain. She buried her face in her hands. She was alone now. Truly alone. She didn't have Pete anymore. Nor did she have Carolyn.

Then Carolyn's hand touched her arm.

"I'm sorry," Luce sobbed. "I'm so sorry."

"I invited her to my party," Carolyn said.

Cally stared, her eyes wide with astonishment. "You what?"

"I invited her to my party."

Down the hall at the water fountain, she could see Luce, her face strained and worried.

"How could you?" Cally hissed.

"She's really sorry about everything that happened."

"And that's supposed to make everything better?" Cally snapped. "Her stupid little apology is supposed to erase the whole past?"

"Cally, I think we ought to give her a chance."

"*You* give her a chance!"

"But I don't want to lose you as a friend," said Carolyn.

Cally's face hardened. "I bet you don't," she said ferociously. "You always liked her better anyway. The first stupid apology she utters, you're falling all over yourself trying to get me to forgive her. Well, forget it. I'm not interested!"

"But, Cally . . . "

"No way!" She slammed her locker door.

"Cally, be reasonable . . . "

"You be reasonable for a change! You think about what

she did. And don't even bother to talk to me until you come to your senses!" She wheeled and stalked away.

Every time Cally looked at his face, she wanted to burst into tears. The skin under his left eye was all puffed up. A gauze bandage covered six stitches on his right eye. But he refused to brood about it. With half his mouth he even smiled.

"What's the matter with you?" Cally demanded. "You think it's funny to get beaten up like that?"

He shook his head.

"Then what are you grinning for? The guy jumped you. He kicked you when you were down."

It happened the week before Carolyn's party. Cally sat in the stands alone this time. Carolyn was at the game with Luce and Mark. Mark had waved Cally over, but she had turned her back, pretending she didn't see.

Tension hung in the air as the game started. Cally held her breath, counting the minutes, and was relieved when halftime came. Orlando flashed her a smile before he left the court, and she thought maybe she was being ridiculous. Maybe nothing was going to happen.

Cally stared straight ahead; she made a point of not looking over to where Carolyn sat with Mark and Luce. Then, when the team came back into the gym for the second half, something happened. She wasn't even sure what. It looked as though Orlando tripped. It was possible that he was pushed. A guy from the other team was coming in behind him and he had a funny smirk on his face as Orlando lurched forward and knocked into Pete. Pete turned around and snarled. Cally's heart stopped.

The crowd gasped. Then Coach Deacon stepped forward between the two of them. Pete backed down.

Cally relaxed slightly when the game started, but she could see Pete was egging Orlando on. He played close to him, even though it was clear from the coach's signals that he wasn't supposed to be where he was. Then, when Orlando went for a catch and Pete knocked into him, Orlando butted Pete with his elbow. That's when Pete started punching and, when he had Orlando down, kicked him hard in the face.

"The way I look at it," Orlando said later, his speech slurred by the swelling on his face, "I made progress."

Cally had been speechless. Since when was a beating progress?

"Yeah," said Orlando. "This time it was just Pete. This time the rest of the guys didn't jump on me too. And this time I didn't get suspended."

"They should have expelled Pete," Cally said, "instead of just suspending him from school for a week. At least he was kicked off the team."

"Yeah," said Orlando, "but you can't always get what you want."

She couldn't understand why he was being so calm about it.

"And I'm not going to Carolyn's stupid party," said Cally.

Orlando studied her for a few moments.

"Carolyn's your friend," he said again. "You should go."

"Carolyn is *not* my friend. She's Luce's friend."

"Cally, I think you should go to the party and make up with your friends. You have to give people a second chance."

Cally was getting angrier and angrier. She couldn't understand why he was saying any of this.

"Aren't you the guy who was going to leave school because of the way people were treating *you?*" she snapped.

"I didn't leave. And I don't think you should leave your friends on account of the way they treated me. People change, you know."

"Luce has always been the way she is. She's never really liked me. She always liked Carolyn better, and Carolyn liked her better."

"So what you're saying is, this has nothing to do with me. This has more to do with your past relationship with Carolyn and Luce. You're jealous of Luce, right? You're pissed off with Carolyn because she was so quick to forgive Luce. Well, I'm going to that party, even if you're not."

"Go ahead," she said. "I don't care."

She was sitting beside him on the sofa in his rec room, and she was glowering at him. But he wasn't glowering back. Instead, he slipped an arm around her shoulder and pulled her closer.

"I'd kiss you," he said, "if I didn't think it would hurt so much."

Cally sighed. She was still mad, but she snuggled a little closer to him, then leaned over and kissed him gently on the cheek.

"Cally, there's something I have to tell you."

She pulled back. She could feel it, a knot in the pit of her stomach that felt like someone was pulling it tighter and tighter. Whenever you heard those words spoken in that tone, you knew it was going to be trouble.

"We're moving," he said.

"Moving?" No. It couldn't be. She saw the room swimming before her eyes. How could he be moving?

"Not till the end of the school year," he continued, looking at a shelf of books across the room. "My dad got a job in New York."

"You're leaving," she said, her voice flat and dull.

"I think you should make up with your friends," he said. "You should have someone after I've left. It will make it easier on you."

She wanted to run from the room, run across the yard to her own house and her own room. But somehow she couldn't move. All she could do was snuggle in his arms and cry.

"You're coming and that's that," Carolyn said.

Luce had nodded, but she didn't feel as confident about it as Carolyn seemed to. "What about Cally?" she asked.

"Cally told me yesterday she was going to come. She said she was sorry for getting so mad at me."

"What did she say about me?"

Carolyn shrugged. "She didn't actually say anything."

"Does she know I'm going to be there?"

"Yes."

As Luce dressed for the party, her stomach churned. Cally was going to be there. Orlando was going to be there. She hadn't spoken to Cally in months. At first she hadn't wanted to, not while she was with Pete. And when it was over between them, Cally had not wanted to speak to her.

"I'm going now," she called to her mother, then she pulled the door shut behind her and started down the

151

walk. She was half a block from Carolyn's house when a hand fell on her shoulder, startling her, making her jump. She spun around.

"Pete!"

Pete was staring down at her, his eyes burning into hers. "Where you off to?" he asked.

"That's none of your business," she snapped. But she didn't feel as fierce as she was trying to sound. She was afraid of Pete now, afraid of what he could do when he was angry, and afraid he might be angry at her.

"Then I'll make it my business," he said. "I bet you're going to Carolyn's."

She stared at him, wondering how on earth he knew.

"Carolyn's having a party," he said. "Funny thing, I just happened to be going by the house and I noticed her mother leaving. Seems like her mother trusts her to have this party without any adult supervision. Sounds like fun, doesn't it?"

"Well, I guess you'll never know," said Luce. "You weren't invited."

"But you were?" Pete didn't wait for an answer. "Funny, eh? You're going. Your little pal Cally is there already with her boyfriend. Funny company you're keeping these days, Luce."

She stared at him, then turned angrily away. But he grabbed her by the arm and wouldn't let go.

"Pete!"

He smiled. "I got nothing to do. Maybe I'll just come along with you."

"Nobody wants you there."

"Nobody told me that," he said.

"You can't come, Pete."

But he was coming. He was walking up Carolyn's front path, up the steps to the door, and when Luce didn't make a move for it, he reached out and pressed the bell.

Carolyn answered. Her mouth dropped open when she saw Pete standing there with Luce. Anger flickered across her face. She glanced at Luce.

"I didn't ask him to come," Luce said desperately. "Honest."

Carolyn nodded. She shifted her gaze back to Pete. "Get out of here, Pete," she said. "You're not invited."

Pete pushed right by her.

Luce followed. "Pete," she called.

Pete pushed his way into the house, his boots dripping snow all over the carpet. He marched into the living room and stood there, surveying the scene. People were dancing to the music and hanging around the food table. In one corner Carolyn's Greatgran sat in an armchair, her head moving vaguely in time with the music.

"We've got to get him out of here," Luce hissed.

"I'll get Mark," said Carolyn. "He's in the kitchen."

Luce saw Orlando at the far end of the house, dancing with Cally, and they both turned to stare at her and Pete. They think we're together, she thought with horror. They think I brought him here. She stepped forward to say something. Cally was staring at her, hating her. And Pete was reaching out for Orlando now, pulling him back from Cally.

"Get out of here, Pete," said Orlando.

"You and I have business," said Pete, pulling roughly on Orlando's arm, trying to jerk him towards the door. But Orlando resisted.

Luce glanced around frantically. Where was Carolyn?

Where was Mark? She moved forward to try to grab Pete, but he shook her off viciously without even looking at her.

Suddenly the old lady in the corner, Carolyn's Greatgran, stood up and said, "I think we need a little music."

Everyone looked over to see Greatgran slip a record onto the turntable. The needle hit the record with a whining sound, and strange, old-fashioned music started to play.

"Greatgran!"

Carolyn was coming in with Mark. She hurried over to Greatgran, while Mark confronted Pete.

"You're not welcome here," he said sharply. "Suppose you beat it."

"Suppose you butt out," said Pete. He gave Mark a little shove.

"Kathleen," said Greatgran, smiling over at Carolyn, "come on, let's dance."

Luce looked at Carolyn, then at Cally. "Who's Kathleen?"

Cally shrugged.

Greatgran took Carolyn by the hand and led her over to the boys. "Come on, Kathleen," she said, "let's get some of these big strong men to dance with us." She reached out and took Pete by the hand.

Pete stared at her. His face turned red as she began to waltz with him, oblivious to the fact that the record wasn't even playing a waltz. She also seemed unaware that Pete was making no effort to dance. The longer she kept him in her grip, swirling around and around, her face pressed close to his, the redder he became.

Carolyn looked at Mark, who gazed back at her and nodded. Then she stepped forward and took Orlando by the hand and began to dance with him. Luce watched them a moment, and then, as if drawn by some invisible hand, she crossed over to Carolyn and tapped her on the shoulder. "Mind if I cut in?"

Orlando began to dance awkwardly with her. When Pete saw that, he let out a howl and jerked away from Greatgran. Mark jumped forward and caught her and guided her back into her chair. Pete snapped off the record player, then turned and ripped Luce away from Orlando.

She faced him with a calmness she could not quite believe. "I think you'd better leave, Pete," she said in a loud, clear voice. "We don't want you here."

Pete looked around the room at Mark and Orlando, at Carolyn, Cally, Luce and the rest of the guests. No one moved. Finally he made a sound of disgust. Then he pushed roughly through the crowd and stormed out of the house.

Carolyn glanced over at Greatgran, who was standing a little behind the crowd, smiling.

With every step they took, Cally felt more and more like crying. Because every step she took with him was one last step she would ever take with him. In twelve hours Orlando would be gone.

She clung to his hand as she walked up the street and nodded to Mr. and Mrs. Curran, who were on their knees, digging in their flower beds. She held her head high as she passed the corner of the street where Pete lived. He wouldn't see them, but she held her head up anyway. When they drew even to the moving van outside Orlando's house, she brushed a tear from her eye.

"I'm going to miss you," she whispered.

He wrapped both arms around her and held her tightly. She heard his heart beating softly in his chest. His kiss was light and warm on her forehead. She wound her arms around his waist and wished for once that summer had never come.